SUMMARY

All Hallows, 1925

Vi Wakefield decides it is time to embrace the fun. She's arranging a scavenger hunt with prizes, specialty cocktails, and costumes.

What she doesn't expect is a series of pranks that ends in a body. Once again, Vi, Jack, and friends are faced with a body, a series of mean and quite dangerous pranks, and the baffling cruelties of mankind. Will they be able to discover what is happening and why, or will this criminal escape into the night?

MURDER ON ALL HALLOWS

A VIOLET CARLYLE HISTORICAL MYSTERY

BETH BYERS

For my Noah.
You're one of my greatest joys.

CHAPTER 1

"Ginny, darling, I find myself both appalled and delighted by your presence." Violet cupped her ward, Ginny, by the face and soundly kissed both cheeks. "You look fabulous for a criminal."

"They deserved it," Ginny said flatly, sniffing once. "It's not my fault."

She tilted her dark head and glanced about with inquisitive eyes. There was not a single gram of guilt in her gaze. In fact, if anything, Ginny was challenging. Violet hid her instinctive reaction and watched as Ginny's gaze flicked from person to person.

First she looked at Violet's twin, Victor, and his wife, Kate. They were each holding one of their twin babies. From them, Ginny's gaze moved to Lila and Denny and on to Jack. Rita was the last person that Ginny paused on. She didn't know Rita as well, and their last friend—Hamilton Barnes—was at work.

"I believe," Violet said carefully, "that when you take a girl by the hair, drag her through the halls, and shove her face into the sink to wash out her mouth with soap you can no longer claim that it was not your fault."

Ginny shrugged and did another one of those sniffs. Violet thought that might, in fact, be an imitation of Vi and her friends. "It's not like I didn't warn Dorothy. 'Never call me guttersnipe again.' I had said it time and again. So often that she mouthed it with me. It was time for consequences."

"I agree with Ginny," Denny said, sniffing. "It was time for consequences."

"I agree as well," Rita said carefully, eyeing Violet. "Though perhaps the consequences should have been less violent."

"I might have done the same," Victor admitted and then winked at Ginny.

Violet turned on them with a dark look. Only Rita held up her hands in surrender.

"I'm not saying that Dorothy Poppington isn't a horrendous creature," Violet tried, but Ginny had quite a powerfully sarcastic snort.

"She is!" Ginny inserted and *sniffed*.

"I'm not saying that she didn't deserve consequences," Violet said again very carefully, controlling all sniffs, snorts, winks, and lifted brows.

"She did."

Thank goodness Ginny didn't sniff again, Violet thought, as she was about to smack her ward on the back of her head.

"But it wasn't your place," Violet told Ginny flatly. "You cannot manhandle and assault your peers. You needed to report the problem to the teachers."

"I did," Ginny told Violet. "Miss Entley witnessed the entire event and did nothing. She didn't even scold Dorothy. I swear she laughed, though I didn't see it. I *did* see the other girls smiling her way. Dorothy's henchwomen, I mean."

"She did what now?" Victor asked, gaze narrowed. He had leaned forward, and the cool threat in his voice had baby Agatha squirming.

"Nothing." Ginny lost her cool as she snapped, voice low. "She did *nothing.*"

Violet took a long breath in, fists curling. She rose and left the house, walking down to the street. Violet didn't even take her coat or hat. She was wearing a gray, pleated dress, gray silk stockings, and simple gray shoes. Her hair was held back with a silver pin on the side. It had been an appropriate dress for a morning with the family.

Thankfully, it was a short drive through the city to the ladies club where Mrs. Partridge, who ran the school that Ginny attended, stayed while in London. The Partridge woman was, after all, staying at Violet's own invitation.

Violet strode up the steps and past the attendant at the door. Violet rarely visited the Piccadilly Ladies Club despite being a member, but the staff knew her all the same.

"Where is Mrs. Partridge?"

The girl heard the cool fury in Violet's voice. "The dining room, my lady."

Vi stalked into the dining room and found Mrs. Partridge sitting at a table with three other ladies. "Oh! Violet, dear. How nice to see you. I was just telling these ladies about your Ginny and our hopes to add more scholarship students."

Violet took a seat, noting the reporter, Emily Allen, at the table. They were not friends—not even close—but the Allen woman enjoyed publishing a good story.

Violet nodded once and only at Miss Allen, who arched her brow. To the others, Violet said flatly, "Ginny is not a scholarship student. I pay rather significantly for her to attend. In fact, I believe that my brother and I donated rather a lot to the school for you to even consider her acceptance."

Mrs. Partridge blushed and stumbled. "Well, you are her benefactress, of course. Her scholarship provider as it were. She's come so far. I believe that other children can be similarly—"

"Bullied?" Violet demanded. "Treated as lesser though I paid significantly more for her to attend? I told you flatly when I placed her in your school I was trusting you with her. That she had a terrible burden of a beginning. I believe I stated quite clearly that my brother and I consider Ginny our family. We even gave her our name. My father, the *earl*, considers Ginny family. My stepmother, who likes no one, likes Ginny Carlyle. Yet—"

"This is neither the time nor the place to discuss your *street* ward, Mrs. Wakefield," Mrs. Partridge interrupted, omitting the title that she preferred to use whenever possible. Mrs. Partridge looked down her significantly pointy nose at Violet, but Vi had been looked at thus by her own stepmother for the entirety of her life.

Violet shifted in the way she did when she put on the persona of the earl's daughter—a persona she avoided. "Oh, I *am* sorry. I was confused by your lies. Let's be clear, then, this is the time you've set aside to lie to the rich women of *my* club and tell them that you accept and encourage young women when you do not? You seek to manipulate them with the story of my ward while she was forced to defend herself in your *hallowed* halls."

Mrs. Partridge's gaze narrowed. "Your ward is a street rat thief who torments the other children, jealous of her betters."

Violet rose, a cold smile on her face. "You are a cold, cruel woman without the imagination to see what lies ahead. Let me help you. Dorothy Poppington will marry a drunkard who doesn't love her. He'll burn through her fortune, and when she's penniless she'll be a burden on the people around her, but she'll still believe herself better than you."

Mrs. Partridge put her hand over her chest.

"While Ginny Carlyle with her intelligence, kindness, bravery, and friends will be a successful woman capable of doing anything she wants. But, here's the rub, she will be better than you then. She is better than you now. She was better than you when she was a hungry orphan taking care of her sick grandmother and still willing to risk herself to save Isolde Carlyle."

"Don't think you can bring her back to my school. She's a…a…hoodlum!"

Violet slowly smiled. "Do you remember our contract? Because it was specific. You should read the details of it once again. You should *remember* that the funds I provided were not a donation. You sold your soul, Partridge, to be able to use my name and accept my ward. Consider me the devil calling your bill due."

Marissa Partridge paled.

"I'll be taking control of the school, or you'll be returning my funds. I believe the contract gives you three days. Those start now. Enjoy your brunch, ladies."

Violet met Emily Allen's gaze as it lifted. "Perhaps we may have a meeting later, Lady Violet?"

"Indeed," Violet nodded. She didn't care for Jack's one-time fiancée, but Emily took her position as a reporter seriously. And her paper would gobble up the news of Lady Violet, her ward, and the school Violet did not want to own or run.

Violet was vindictive when it came to those she loved. Therefore, she both made the appointment with Miss Allen to Mrs. Partridge's stuttering distress and then crossed to the club management and revoked the invitation for Mrs. Partridge to stay at the ladies club.

Violet left the club and found Jack outside with her coat and hat.

"What are we going to do?" He pressed a kiss on

Violet's forehead before he plonked her hat on her head and held the coat for her.

"I don't know." Violet peered past Jack's broad shoulders to the street, pressing her fingers to her temples. She told him of the meeting, and his fury was a heat Violet could warm herself against. "I'd like to just keep her home, but I—Jack? Is that the right thing to do? I can't trust that fool Partridge with Ginny again, but do I trust another school? I can't actually take the school over, and Partridge will fight me. Even without that stupid woman running the school, it's not as if idiots like Dorothy Poppington are unique to any school we'd send Ginny to."

Jack shook his head and then carefully said, "You know, Ginny might have her own opinions."

Violet pressed her face into his chest. Caring about young people and having no idea how to help them was more difficult than anything else she'd faced. She had *no idea* how her Aunt Agatha had raised her and Victor with so much grace. Had Aunt Agatha paced the halls, worrying over them? Had she been sleepless? Had she been too sick with worry to eat or focus her mind on anything else? What Violet wouldn't give to throw herself in Aunt Agatha's lap and ask what to do about Ginny.

"When I think about it," Violet glanced up at him through her lashes, "my mind is an utter blank. All I can think is that I'm not ready for this—"

He laughed and then stiffened. His gaze was fixed beyond her. Violet turned and found Emily Allen standing on the steps of the club watching them.

"Em," Jack said, nodding once. He was as stiff as steel and Violet tangled their fingers together.

"Jack," Emily Allen said, nodding once. Her gaze moved to Violet, landing for a moment on their hands and then traveling to Violet's face. "I was wondering if I might speak with your ward as well. Or is she adopted?"

"Officially, she's adopted," Violet said. "She prefers the word ward because she doesn't want to feel as though she abandoned her original family. They were good people and worthy of remembering and acknowledging."

"Then why didn't she remain a ward?"

"My father convinced her to become a Carlyle."

"The earl?" Miss Allen asked.

Violet contained her vicious sniff, snort, wink—all of the things that Ginny had picked up that Violet now regretted immensely. Instead, Violet nodded once and hoped that she didn't seem too stiff.

"You can interview Ginny with me there," Jack told Emily. "Violet is in the middle of a book deadline."

It was an out-and-out lie, and Violet didn't care for Miss Allen's slow grin. Vi wasn't worried about Jack's intentions, so she bit back any reaction that would give Miss Allen an idea of Vi's worries. She ignored Miss Allen's flirting, and Jack's replies and watched the traffic go by. It was nearly All Hallows, Violet thought. They should have a party while they worked out all the issues associated with Ginny and her schooling.

Violet considered that they could easily have that

party that Denny had half-imagined. A rented museum. Actors playing ghouls and other creatures. Fantastic costumes. Exotic cocktails. Something to distract herself from being entirely inept as the parental adult in Ginny's life.

"WHAT'S GOING to happen to me?" Ginny asked that evening as she brushed Holmes's coat. Rouge was in the basket with her four puppies and unwilling to abandon them for a snuggle.

"I—" Violet wanted to explain in detail about what had happened with the Partridge woman, but at what point did she need to hold things back? To not put her worries on Ginny? To tell Ginny, I need you to behave in this particular way learning from what I say, not what I do? "I am not going to send you back to that school."

Ginny's shoulders dropped a little as though in relief. Her face was nearly emotionless, and it seemed almost as though Violet had lifted a weight off of her ward's shoulders. "What am I going to do?"

Violet pressed her lips together and admitted, "I don't know."

"Would you object terribly to my staying here?"

Violet had to hold back her instinctive answer and instead consider. "Do you want to go to university?"

Ginny nodded.

"You'll have to deal with the likes of Dorothy Poppington then, you know."

Ginny took in a slow breath and held it. She didn't say anything else, but her dark eyes were wide, fixed, and filled with an emotion that Vi couldn't quite read.

Praying silently that she wasn't making a terrible mistake, Violet said, "It's much more difficult, though, to avoid those who aren't worth your time or attention in a boarding school than at university. Things will be different there than boarding school."

Ginny's hands curled into fists, but she was otherwise quiet. Violet's gaze landed on the fists and then moved past to the floor so Ginny wouldn't hide her reactions.

"We can try you staying here and studying with a tutor, but I do think we should look into another school for you. Maybe you'd like to do the research and see if there is something that feels right?"

Ginny asked, "I can choose?"

Violet nodded, hoping she wasn't making a terrible mistake.

"What if I can't find one?"

"Then you had better study hard with your tutor."

Ginny contained a crow of triumph and Violet contained an instant desire to change her mind, afraid she'd made the wrong choice. Considering, she watched as Denny and Victor discussed the possibilities of cocktails while she leaned back to consider her own costume.

CHAPTER 2

*V*iolet woke the next day to Jack getting up and dressing for brunch with Emily Allen. She sat up and watched him dress. He disappeared into the bath, and she pulled her journal from the nightstand while he washed and shaved. When he returned to the bedroom, he was wearing a light tan morning suit with Vi's favorite blue tie. He smelled of cologne and he was carefully adjusting his jacket.

"Good morning," Violet said, raising an intentional brow.

He examined her face as she stared at him. "Are you jealous?"

She shook her head and then asked, "Did you want me to be?"

He grinned suddenly, a surprised laugh escaping him as he admitted, "Perhaps a little."

Violet groaned and flopped onto his side of the

bed, curling herself around his pillow while he smoothed his hair back in the mirror. "You look handsome, you giant troll."

"Em thinks I'm handsome," Jack told Violet and watched her snuggle into his pillow. "I might end up being jealous of my own pillow."

"I would tell you I was going to rage shop, but you wouldn't care."

"By all means, rage shop."

Violet lifted a brow.

"Did I just dare you to do something?"

"Yes," Violet told him. "You certainly did. I'm going to win."

"Are you?" The idle question was enough to spur along her frivolity.

She threw his pillow at him and rolled the other way out of the bed, running into the bedroom. She reached the door, glanced back, and then said, "I'm going to spend a shocking amount of money today. On ridiculous things. Your back teeth will ache."

"I doubt it."

She grinned evilly, shut the bath door in his face, and turned on the water to the tub. Violet haphazardly tossed salts and oils into the bath and dropped into the bubbles, dunking under the water.

She lingered until Jack and Ginny were well gone, and then dressed with an eye towards smuggling Kate with her. What would it take to get Kate away from both the babies and Victor? Or! Was Victor a chance?

Violet wrote a note to her brother, sent it with a maid, and then dressed in a soft blue day dress, silk stockings and pretty shoes, and put a broach at her throat along with bangles on her wrists. She wanted Turkish coffee, a scone with clotted cream and black-berry jam, thick bacon, and a long day without wondering exactly how she was going to avoid ruining Ginny.

Violet found Victor in the breakfast room with the coffee already poured.

"You're an excellent brother," she told him as she filled her plate. The kitchens hadn't left them wanting, and she joined her brother, who had loaded his own plate with all the same things along with a pile of fried tomatoes and sausages.

"I know. I am the best brother."

She nudged him. "So, are we escaping?"

"Jack challenged you. You've called upon me. The twins are terrifying as they teethe. Also, I have an idea. It's a bit regurgitated, but I found a shocking place a few days ago, and I think we can do it."

"A place?"

He grinned at her with that same smirking expression she used so often. Perfect, she thought. She had no idea what he was talking about, but she knew that his excited expression would match just how she would feel when he finally revealed all.

THE HOUSE that Victor brought her to could only be described as fantastic. It seemed to be a cross between a Victorian mansion and a castle. The shape was all peaks and curlicues, but it was made out of stone and iron. The top of the house was covered with fierce gargoyles that half-scared Violet even though she was only partially wicked.

"I love it."

Victor grinned. "Wait until you see the inside."

Violet followed him up the steps, hand on his elbow, and as they approached a servant opened the door before they even reached for the handle.

"Mr. Carlyle."

Violet glanced at Victor. "Why do they know you?"

"Have you noticed that this place is a few short blocks from our houses?"

Violet shook her head. "How did I not know it was here?"

"I found it walking Gin and escaping the girls as they were screaming about their teeth."

"You're so old!" Violet told him. "It's like you're a completely different human than the man I knew. Father would say this is what happens from fornicating."

Victor pulled Violet's hair and then admitted, "I suppose we did that."

"You did."

"Babies happen after marriage as well."

"I don't know what you're talking about," Violet said with an evil smirk as they walked inside, and then she gasped.

The chandelier overhead was black iron. There were crossed, giant black axes mounted on the wall. Violet spun, glancing into the parlor and took in the display cases. She didn't even wait for Victor to speak to the man who had let them in. She rudely walked into the parlor and gazed into the case. It was full of miniature skulls. A part of her recoiled and then she faced to her twin.

"Is this whole place like this?"

"The occult?" He nodded. "Items for séances, Ouija boards, fertility statues, altars for death deities. Generally filled in with weapons for murder, replicas of the guillotine, maps of the black plague. A rather large and fabulous ballroom and a willingness to let for the right price."

"Which is?"

"The purchase of an antique sword believed to be used by Vlad the III."

Violet grinned. "Can we put on it that it was donated by Jack Wakefield?"

He grinned back. "Why would we do anything else?"

Violet followed Victor through the museum to a chocolate shop, to the costume shop, and then pulled him with her into a jewelry store.

"Violet," Victor said carefully.

She turned on him. He lifted both hands slowly.

"What do you have that is ridiculous and expensive?" she asked the clerk.

The man behind the counter eyed Violet's wedding ring, her earbobs, and the gold bangles. He grinned avariciously.

"Something for the season?" she added.

His eyes brightened even further and he went to

the locked cabinet, pulling out a case at the back. Slowly, he opened a black velvet case.

Inside were six black diamond spider hairpins, each with ruby red eyes. Violet gasped as Victor groaned.

"You know," the man said, "I have a quite nice choker that will go well with these."

"I like chokers," Violet told him.

It was a black diamond choker with a few red rubies mixed in.

"There are matching bracelets."

"Yes," Violet said.

"No, Vi. You should…"

She lifted a brow at him.

"I suppose you can afford it."

"I suppose I can."

She left with the necklace, the hairpins, the bangles, a matching spider ring for her forefinger, and black diamond earbobs.

"Between the museum, the costumes, the other dress, and the jewelry, you have definitely surpassed even what Jack would expect."

"He knew I would."

"I suppose you didn't surpass those expectations then."

"I suppose not," Violet admitted. "I could get another dog?"

"You have four puppies you haven't decided if you're keeping or finding homes for."

"Beatrice is taking one, Lila is taking one, Rita is taking one, Father wants one. They all have homes where I can come and visit and love on them, but they aren't staying with us."

"This time."

Violet grinned evilly and shrugged. Her brother wasn't, however, wrong.

"WHAT DO YOU THINK SHE BOUGHT?" Ginny asked Jack. She lifted a brow and smirked.

He glanced at her and laughed as he brought his bright blue Rolls-Royce into the traffic. It was brand new, and Jack just might love it.

"A dress."

Ginny snorted.

Jack noted how she'd perfectly imitated Violet. "Violet was sure she'd shock me, so it will be something you couldn't guess."

Ginny's laughing scoff was an echo of Rita when she was tormenting Ham. Jack rubbed the back of his neck. Breakfast with Em had been bad enough. Breakfast with Em while Ginny reflected all of their bad habits, it was possible that their entire group needed some sort of heart-to-heart intervention.

"Do you think your friend will say bad things about me?"

Jack hesitated. Emily had certainly twisted things about Violet in the past, but if he had to guess, he very much doubted that she'd do the same to Ginny.

The truth was Ginny's story was compelling. She spoke clearly about the abuse she'd received from the other girls and the way the teachers had reacted. Jack *knew* Emily. He'd seen the spark of anger in her gaze.

"She said she was going to talk to the other girls," Ginny said, as she stared out the window, sounding for once like a schoolgirl. "They'll lie."

"People lie to reporters all of the time," Jack told Ginny. "Em is good at ferreting out the truth."

"How do you know her?" Ginny asked.

Jack turned his gaze to the road and shifted in order to distract her from the question. He'd been engaged once to Emily. He'd thought he loved her, and he wasn't sure that Ginny was capable of under-standing that you could misidentify love, make life plans, have them all fall apart, and give up thoughts of family and love.

The idea that men didn't want families and homes just wasn't true. Jack had wanted a home of his own since he'd enjoyed the love and care of his childhood home. He just thought he'd never have one when Emily cheated on him.

"We thought we loved each other once," he told Ginny carefully. "We were wrong." Ginny was gaping, jaw dropped, eyes wide, and Jack had to laugh. It was laugh or wince. "Emily might not even be able to talk to the other girls."

"Mrs. Partridge sent a good number of them down," Ginny muttered. "She does that for half-excuses whenever they want to go home. I doubt their letters home were anything like mine."

Jack rubbed his forehead and then pulled the auto in front of the house. He got out, walked around to open the door for Ginny, and told her, "If they're in London, Emily can talk to them. Your school isn't too far away to visit either."

"Is what Miss Allen said true? Does Violet really own a part of the school?"

Jack nodded. "She does. She bought into it so you could go there."

Ginny bit her bottom lip and then ran inside. Jack followed, hoping he hadn't said the wrong things. Violet was right. Being expected to guide young people was enough to make you feel like a ripe idiot who shouldn't have been allowed to leave school.

"Geoffrey is home," Ginny said over her shoulder. "We're going to meet at the museum."

"Geoffrey?" Jack asked. Violet's younger half-brother was less of a wart than he had been, but it hadn't been entirely rid of him.

"He got sent down as well."

Jack rolled his eyes and then tried to smooth his face into evenness. These children were challenging his capacity to be enigmatic.

CHAPTER 3

*I*t took Violet three days to arrange the rental of the small museum with the purchase of the weapon. It was going to be the most absolutely fabulous All Hallows party. When she'd walked the halls, as she had four more times, she'd found appropriately spooky armor lining one large hall. In one display room, she found old swords and axes mounted on the walls with masks that had been intended to terrify mixed in. There had been an entire room that contained paintings, sculptures, and odd metal creations of demons, gargoyles, and other terrible creatures.

"Yes," Denny said when she announced her plans of a party, scavenger hunt, costume contest. "Yes, I'm going to be something horrible. I need a mask. I need a costumer. I need—" He bounced a little before he demanded, "Can it be a masquerade?"

Violet nodded. "Beatrice is writing the invitations. They'll be sent by tomorrow. Costumes and masks required."

"I want to be a spider," Ginny announced. "May I go?"

Before Violet could answer, Denny cut in, "Of course you can. With all eight legs?"

"Certainly," Ginny answered. She sniffed once and lifted an imperious brow. "Anything else would be inaccurate and pathetic."

"We'll need to go shopping," Lila said lazily. She looked down at her baby mound and sighed, "I believe I shall go as a beef roast."

"Oh luvie." Denny gave his wife an evil grin and then an advanced wince that said he knew he shouldn't be saying what came next. "You could be an oversized turnip or a sweet, round Brussels sprout."

Lila sat up. "You hate Brussels sprouts."

"But I wouldn't," Denny said as if he were being clever, "if you were one."

Lila's gaze narrowed and Denny rose and fled the room. They could hear the tap of his shoes clicking down the wood halls. The door to the library opened and closed, and Violet glanced at Lila. Her expression hadn't adjusted and she still stared after Denny as if plotting.

"Listen," Violet said carefully. "You're beautiful."

Lila grinned. "I know."

"I think the growing baby is cute," Ginny said. "You...glow? It's like your skin is shinier and your hair. There is something different besides the baby."

"Go read a Shakespeare play or something." Violet frowned at Ginny. "Or, I don't know. I feel irresponsible having you just watch us lounge about. Imagine us being productive. Oh! Go find Beatrice in her office and help her."

Ginny's gaze lighted and she hurried out of the parlor.

"We really are terrible examples," Lila said. "We should be ashamed of ourselves."

"Are you upset about what Denny said?"

She shook her head and grinned evilly. "It's good that he fears—"

A high-pitched scream cut off Lila and she jumped to her feet as though she weren't quite pregnant.

"Denny!"

"Denny?" Violet asked, but Lila had darted across the parlor and was to the door when the high-pitched scream repeated.

"Denny!" Lila rushed to the library.

"Don't come in!" he squeaked.

"Denny!"

"Don't!"

Lila's eyes widened. "He's serious. That's his serious voice."

"That's also a terrified child scream." Violet glanced back when she heard Jack running down the hall. Before he could ask a question, Denny screamed again.

"Go away, Lila!" Denny said once his screaming ended. Hargreaves arrived a moment later. "Save yourself!"

"Denny?" Jack called.

"Save me! Don't let Lila come in! Bloody hell, Jack, bring your guns!"

Jack carefully opened the library door. The first thing they saw was Denny standing on one of the overstuffed chairs. He had one leg up tucked towards his chest and his eyes were rolling wildly as he clutched his throat and chest.

"S-s-s-snake! Adder!"

Jack pushed Violet into Lila and shut the door after him.

"I'll find something to contain it," Hargreaves said and rushed to the kitchen.

"Snake?" Vi asked, glancing at Lila. She lifted her brow and immediately dropped it when she remembered Ginny doing just that over her marmalade and toast.

"Denny is afraid of them." Lila frowned. "Terrified really." After another long moment she added, "Aren't adders poisonous?"

Hargreaves returned with a box and a broom and quickly entered the library, closing the door tightly behind him. After far too many moments, Jack cursed loud enough to have Violet worried, but he called, "It's all right now."

Violet walked into the library and was shocked to see Jack holding the box that moved with an agitated occupant. "Is it poisonous?"

Jack nodded. "But adders aren't aggressive. This fellow just needs to be released somewhere safe."

Violet shook her head, walking around him in a wide circle. "It needs to go!"

"It does!" Denny was still on the chair.

Violet frowned deeply. "Our dogs could have easily come in here."

"*I* came in here!" Denny squeaked. He was eyeing every inch of the floor as if there could be another one. Hargreaves was circling the room with his broom, knocking it against the furniture to scare out any other snakes.

"That adder would have killed Rouge or Holmes," Vi said in a tight voice.

"I agree," Jack said. "There's no way an adder got into our library on accident, Vi. This was a nasty, intentional act."

Denny had pulled Lila onto the chair with him. "What if there's another one?"

"What if we'd laid one of the babies on the floor?" Violet demanded. "What if—"

"Take a deep breath, Vi," Jack told her. He nodded at the bell and she crossed the floor to ring it.

Violet rang the bell and left the library. Her dogs and the babies at the forefront of her mind, Violet hurried down the hallway towards the kitchens where Rouge's basket with her puppies was kept by the ovens for warmth.

Victor had taken the twins back to his house after Violet had disappeared that morning. Victor's house would be the best choice.

"Ma'am?" one of the maids asked as Violet entered.

Vi whistled for Holmes and then said, "They're going to Victor's for the next little bit."

She paused. Rouge growled at Vi, but it was the protective mama growl and with one "shush," the dog stopped. Violet trailed her finger over the pups. They were all shades of red and white. Like Rouge, most of them were almost entirely a coppery red, but there was one that was predominately white with accenting splashes of red. Each of the puppies welcomed the loves. They were getting big, and sooner or later, Violet needed to decide when to send them to their new homes and how she was going to successfully stop future batches of puppies.

"Send Ginny to my brother's house," Violet called, walking out the back door and through the garden path they'd made between their houses. There was one house between them, but the owner had allowed them a private path when Victor had given the man some untold amount of money. He'd turned the back end of the man's garden into a pretty little alley walkway, only accessible between their two houses. The money had probably been a ridiculous amount, Vi thought, uncaring of the waste.

Vi hurried down the pathway and found Victor in the garden. He took in the sight of Violet holding the basket of puppies and the two dogs barking at Vi's feet. He knew her well and took in her expression of worry and stress without a word needing to be said.

The two of them were, of course, fraternal twins, but they looked like matching coins. They had the same sharp features, clever dark eyes, the same dark hair, the same full lips, and the same expressions that only intensified their alikeness.

"What happened?"

"There was a snake in the library."

Her tone was enough to have him lowering his brows, instantly worried.

"I'm sending you Ginny and the dogs. Keep the twins at your house."

"For a snake?" He accepted the basket of puppies that she held out for him.

"Jack thinks it was a malicious prank. I'm sure he's currently figuring out how it happened."

"Vi—"

The doubt was enough to make her slap his arm. "It was an adder, you fool. There's no way it ended up there by accident."

Victor's face smoothed into cool fury.

"I know," Violet told him, feeling the same cold, painful anger.

Victor helped her bring the dogs inside. They took them up to the nursery where the nanny would be able to keep a careful eye on them along with the babies.

"What about you?" Victor asked. "Are you going to come here too?"

Violet winked at him, snorted, and then sighed deeply.

"I know!" He groaned. "Bloody hell, Vi. Ginny has all of our bad habits. We're terrible examples of humanity. We're raising someone who is—well, she's naturally smarter than we are, certainly, so she'll turn out better than we did. No one likes a snorting, sniffing, sarcastic school girl."

"We like her," Violet said with a sigh that she cut off halfway through. "I've been trying to stop, but I *can't*. It's an affliction."

Victor snorted, and Violet elbowed him gently, so he wouldn't drop the puppies. "Right, we're stopping that."

"Perhaps easing back," Vi admitted.

"I'm not sure we can do better than easing," Victor agreed. "We do spend a lot of time with Denny, and he is an idiot."

Violet followed Victor inside and told Rouge and Holmes to stay. Holmes tried to follow Violet, but she snapped, "Stay."

His big brown eyes looked up at her with a heart-broken expression.

"Stop it."

He whimpered and Violet sniffed, picking him up. He nuzzled his face into her neck, tail wagging. "It'll be all right, baby," she told him, letting him kiss her chin before she turned him over to the nanny and left to his barked cry.

"How did it happen?" Victor asked Jack when they entered the library. Every piece of furniture had been shifted to search for any other snakes and it was being moved back.

"There was a rash of deliveries all at once. One boy

arrived with a box and disappeared before he could be dealt with. No one questioned it with the meat, milk, and bread arriving all at once."

"Must've known where to go," Victor said, stepping into the hall and staring down towards the kitchen. "He would have to have been a sneaky thing to get past your Cook and Hargreaves."

"Indeed." Jack sighed and helped the driver-gardener move the heavy desk back into place. "There's no reason to believe that there was anything else. The door to the library was shut all morning. No snakes could have gotten out of the library. There isn't another one hiding in here."

"Why would someone do this to us?" Violet asked, glancing at Jack.

Jack shook his head, as mystified as Vi. "I have no idea, Vi."

CHAPTER 4

*V*iolet stood on a small stool in her parlor while the fit of her witch's costume was checked before she accepted the final delivery. It was a fitted black dress that had been embroidered with spider webs. The embroidery was accented with small, silver beads just often enough that in the candlelight of the party, they'd twinkle. Her mask, unlike her dress, was terrifying. It had a long green nose and a large mole near the exaggerated cheekbone. It would cover her face entirely so no one would be able to see who she was.

She had a pointed hat wrapped in black silk with a stuffed raven on the brim. Violet preferred to avoid meeting the creature's gaze, so she pulled the hat off as soon as she checked the fit.

"You should wear jet black beads," Lila told Violet.

"With that new black diamond choker. Let's go shopping for jewelry."

"I just did." Violet frowned. "Do you hear that?"

"Cheap jewelry. I can't buy myself heirlooms on a whim," Lila said and yawned. Unlike Kate, Lila very rarely caressed her baby mound, but Vi noted the careful placement of Lila's palm at that particular moment.

"I heard it," the seamstress said, nodding, pins in her mouth. "It's like the skittering of tiny nails. You said you have puppies, right? Perhaps they got out of their box?"

"Aren't the puppies at Victor's?" Lila asked.

Violet carefully stepped down from the stool and crossed the parlor to the hallway. She cautiously opened the door and then—to her shame—screamed like Denny meeting a snake.

Jack burst from the library as Violet cut off her shriek. Lila grabbed Violet's bicep as they stared in horror at the good fifty mice that had been put in through the letter slot.

"Bloody hell!" Jack shouted. "Hargreaves!"

Violet closed her eyes and ran to the front door, swinging it wide. It was a good move as at least some of the mice went fleeing out the opening and down into the street. Violet ignored them even as she stepped up onto the rim of a large stone flower pot to avoid them touching her. She stared down the street and just saw the figure of a person in a long black coat and black hat fleeing around the corner.

"They're already gone," Violet said, glancing back

at Hargreaves. The hallway had emptied of mice, but Violet had little doubt that some were hiding under furniture or behind doors. "We're going to need some cats."

"I'll take care of, Mrs. Vi," Hargreaves said, glancing back at Jack. "What is happening to our home?"

Violet stared at Hargreaves while Jack lifted Violet down.

"I like your costume," Jack said almost absently. "Find us some cats," he said to Hargreaves. "Hire some more servants. Let's see if more eyes solve the problem."

Violet returned to the parlor and found the costumer packing up her things. "S-s-some of them came in here. I have—I have quite a terrible fear of rodents, ma'am. I'm sorry. Your dress looks lovely. It's quite all right as it is."

Violet didn't argue. She sent a maid in to help the woman clear her things out and sent her down to Victor's house to help with Ginny's costume. Violet faced the room. She shivered as she remembered the sound of all those small claws on her wood floors and then glanced at Lila.

Lila had been fitted first and her renaissance princess costume floated about her feet as she stood on a chair.

"A few did come in here."

Violet lifted a brow at Lila and sniffed dramatically

"Stop it," Lila said, shuddering. "I hate mice."

"They're just tiny little animals."

"You screamed like Denny as if it were raining snakes."

"You're on a chair like Denny as if it were flooding snakes."

Lila choked on her laughter and then gestured imperiously for Jack. He crossed to her and she jumped into his arms. "Carry me to the stairs, my liege, and don't tell me if mice can climb stairs. I'm changing and going home to nap in safety."

Violet heard a skittering noise and hurried up the stairs after Lila. Vi wasn't going to be driven from her home, but she had to admit that she was at a bit of a loss. She was nearly certain that skittering noise she'd just heard was entirely in her imagination.

"Get a good half-dozen cats, Hargreaves. Set them on the halls as though we've been invaded by felines. Feel free to issue them muskets for mouses."

"Yes, ma'am."

She ran up the stairs, carefully hung her dress in her closet and changed into a pinky-nude day dress. Violet added several bangles and a pretty gold ring to play with as she paced her bedroom floor. As she paced, she paused to straighten her perfume bottles or the shoes in her wardrobe. Violet paced and thought and paced and thought until she was entirely without an idea of what to do.

Why was this happening to them? *How* were they going to find the culprit? Once could have been a simple prank, but twice? It was like guerrilla warfare with the carefully planned attacks on the unsuspecting household. Someone wasn't going to get away with shoving things through the letter slot again. Someone wasn't going to get away with sneaking in a disgusting package with their regular deliveries, but what was going to happen next?

How did you defend against an unknowable action? Had they enraged someone? Violet immediately thought of Mrs. Partridge, but really—the woman ran a girl's school. She might have a good idea of the effect of pranks, but she was also an adult who had to be above such shenanigans.

As Violet's youngest brother had been sent down from school again, she'd considered him seriously. She *had* asked her father about Geoffrey after the snake prank. Supposedly, he was doing well this year at school, Father had said. Given that Father had been dropping in on Geoffrey at school *without* Lady Eleanor, Vi thought he might be right about Geoffrey.

Would Ginny do this? Violet shook her head immediately. Ginny wasn't stupid. She would never put the dogs or the babies at risk. She might be a schoolgirl, but she wasn't cruel or mean. Especially to Violet.

Vi tapped her finger to her chin. They hadn't owned the house all that long. Perhaps it was a prank directed toward the previous occupants of the house? Vi shrugged off that idea almost immediately. The man who had lived there before with his hangers-on children and grandchildren had been old and kind.

What if it had something to do with one of the cases that Jack worked or Violet had meddled in? She thought back to the last one. It had been a murder and a drug-smuggling enterprise. Violet thought that if someone were out for revenge, it would be a crueler, more violent revenge than rodents through the mail slot.

The case before that one was a woman who had killed her husband. Violet knew all too well that Pamela was in a sanatorium and well along in her pregnancy. The woman would be giving birth any day and, aside from the fact that she was locked away, wouldn't be able to rabbit down the road with the same speed that today's culprit had accomplished.

Violet's mouth twisted. Most of Jack's cases were murderers. They weren't the type for this petty level of revenge, were they? Surely if you'd taken a life once and felt the need for revenge, the next step wouldn't be a snake and mice?

On the other hand they might as well have Hamilton check in on those they'd helped lock up. Perhaps something had happened and they needed to be concerned?

Violet started to make her way back down the stairs and then reconsidered. She changed from her day dress to a solid gray, pleated skirt topped with a white blouse, a blue jumper, and finished with her knee-high black riding boots.

Violet wanted her brother, her husband, and Hamilton Barnes. Jack was in the library, a deep scowl on his face, gaze fixed towards the corner of the library. "There's one over there."

Violet crossed to him, taking a seat on his lap and distracting him from the mouse. He placed a hand on her thigh to hold her to him and noted her boots with a grin.

"Not a bad choice."

"Have you called Ham yet?"

"He's out for lunch."

Violet considered for a moment, and then she and Jack said in almost unison, "Hotel Saffron."

Jack stood, holding Violet in his arms, and found Hargreaves in the hall with a suspiciously bloody bundle in his hands.

"There's one in the library."

"The cats are on their way."

"Bonuses for the staff," Violet announced. "With some sort of special treat as well on their next evening off."

"That's tonight, ma'am," Hargreaves told Violet. "Did you want me to cancel it?"

Violet paused before she answered. "Ah. No. But warn the local constable to keep an eye on our house, please, and lock up with extra precision."

"Yes, ma'am," Hargreaves said. He nodded to Jack, who carried Violet to the front door.

"We're off to Hotel Saffron to find Rita and Ham."

CHAPTER 5

*V*iolet was pretty enough. She had a slim figure, animated features, and a bright smile. Rita, however, was the kind of beautiful that stopped you in your tracks and you remembered later. She was an animated painting from a master artist. Her eyes were large and as blue as the Mediterranean. Her blonde hair was marcelled along her face, and her pink lips were the kind of lush that left another girl envious.

When she frowned, as she was doing at that moment, she frowned so fiercely it was as though an evil queen stepped out of a fairytale and into her body. Only someone magical could be that beautiful and that furious. When Rita stood, picked up her cocktail, and tossed it into Ham's face, Violet winced for them all.

Ham calmly wiped his face as Rita spun and faced her audience.

"You take Ham," Violet said to Jack and then she followed Rita from the dining room to the penthouse suite.

Rita stormed to the lift, shooting Violet a dark look but not kicking her out. From the lift, she stalked down the hall to the double doors at the end and then into her suite. The first room of the suite was a combination parlor and dining area, with a desk in the corner and stacks upon stacks of Rita's favorite books littering chairs, end tables, and shelves.

Rita threw herself on the large, comfortable chair. "I don't want to hear about it."

"About the mice in the letter slot?" Violet asked, taking a seat across from Rita. She calmly called down to room service for ginger wine, Turkish coffee, and sweets.

Rita's rage-filled gaze shifted to confusion. "What now?"

"Mice. Letter slot. At least fifty of them, though I feel that the true horror can only be conveyed by magnifying the number to one hundred."

"Mice?" Rita repeated.

"In the letter slot. Hargreaves is currently acquiring cats."

Rita stared, her beautiful mouth hanging open. "Cats?"

"Like soldier assassins with a special mouse murdering mission. Do you want to go out for cocktails and dancing this evening? I need to pretend as though I didn't have them running over my bare toes."

"Why were your feet bare?"

"I was being fitted for my costume when a strange skittering sound from the front hall filled the air and filled me with an unholy curiosity that ended with unholy fodder for nightmares."

Rita shuddered as Violet continued. "I thought to myself—whoever did this must be right outside. So like a brave general, I waded into the sea of attackers and flung open the door, leaping to the safety of the flower pot rim."

"I can see it now," Rita murmured, rising to open the door for room service. She poured them both oversized glasses of ginger wine.

"Can you?"

"You have a way with words."

"You have a way with drinks," Violet said, accepting her ginger wine, but her mischievous gaze met Rita's. "Almost a—ah…"

"Assaultive?"

"Generous to a *fault*?"

"A storm of gin?"

"A barrage of Bacardi?"

"Stop it," Rita laughed. "Oh, he makes me so mad."

"Well," Violet said carefully, "you showed him."

Rita snorted and Violet held up a hand. "Don't! We're giving up snorts, sniffs, winks, and the emphatic lifting of brows."

Rita's snort turned into choked laughter. "Ginny is a delight."

"She is an excellent impressionist."

"She fits in well."

"She makes us look like fools."

"Perhaps," Rita suggested slyly as she sipped from her ginger wine glass, then set it carefully down to throw herself on the Chesterfield, "we are fools."

"Oh certainly," Violet agreed. "I'd rather prefer, however, for Ginny not to be."

Rita's laughter was muffled as she rolled onto her side and then escaped again as she noticed Violet's boot armor.

"You'd be wearing them too," Violet said, "if it had been you with tiny claws digging into your toes."

Rita propped herself up on her elbow, reached for a chocolate petit four and said agreeably, "I certainly would. Who is doing this to you?"

"I don't know," Violet admitted. "It seems a bit childish for our enemies and a bit too cruel for pranks from friends." Vi paused and told herself not to say it, but she couldn't quite stop herself. "Rather like throwing a drink in Ham's face."

Rita grinned and then callously shrugged as she reached for another petit four. "You aren't going to let it go, are you?"

Violet shook her head, fighting the desire to snort sarcastically.

Rita noted Vi's struggle and laughed into her hand.

"I could gag you," Violet told Rita.

"I could throw my ginger wine into your face as well."

"What did Ham do?"

Rita groaned and rolled onto her back. She threw her arm over her eyes. "Caught me flirting with Mr. Rothstein from America."

BETH BYERS

Violet could not help herself from lifting a brow imperiously. At her silence, Rita raised her arm enough to see Violet's arched look.

"I know! He's handsome and charming and it was just a bit of good fun."

Violet poured herself a cup of Turkish coffee and took a long sip. "So Ham was jealous?" Violet asked.

"He was and he wasn't. He was jealous, and a little hurt —I think—which made me feel terrible. I wasn't very nice because I was feeling so bad and now I feel like a beast. I haven't fully forgiven him, you know. I laid my heart at his feet, and he picked it up and handed it back to me."

Violet winced.

"I know that I came back here to give things a chance, but I just have a giant ball of hurt inside of me, and it hasn't gone away, and sometimes I just want to hit him over and over again."

Violet switched back to her ginger wine, unrepentant of her excess and then, to top it all off, she popped a petit four into her mouth and washed it down with another swallow of ginger wine.

"I'm not going to tell you that you were wrong," Violet told Rita flatly. "If you were waiting for that, you're going to have to take a deep breath and keep on waiting."

Rita groaned. "I'm not sure I *was* wrong for harmlessly flirting. I haven't made Ham one promise. Not one. However, I am sorry for how I acted afterward."

"Maybe you could tell him tonight when we go dancing," Violet said. "Our house is getting locked up tight so the servants can still have their evening off. The cats will hunt, I hope, and I have every intention of drinking enough to forget the sound of mice falling through the letterbox."

Rita dropped her arm and sat up. "I suppose I should."

"Mmm," Violet said carefully, avoiding Rita's gaze.

"It's like I'm trying to drive him away," Rita told Violet. "Why am I doing that? I can't help myself."

"Maybe to see if he'll hand you back your heart?"

Rita scowled and then stood. She noticed the splatter of cocktail on her dress and went into the bedroom. Violet didn't bother to follow Rita as she changed her dress, but there was a knock on the door of the suite. Vi crossed to answer the door and found Jack on the other side.

He lifted an inquiring brow, and Violet reached up and nudged it back into its usual place.

"Are you well?"

Violet nodded and pushed up on her toes to try to see over Jack's shoulder.

"He went back to work."

"Is he upset?"

"He's smelling of gin and going to work, so yes. The woman he loves is furious with him, and he both knows why and also doesn't have a clue as to what is going on."

"Is he—?"

"Is he done? No. I think he might wring her neck, but he's said he won't let go again until she tells him to, and she doesn't tell him to leave, she simply drives him mad."

Violet snorted and then groaned.

"I'm going to leave you here if you're fine," Jack told her.

"I am," Violet said. She pressed a kiss to his cheek and ordered, "Cocktails, dinner, and dancing."

"Certainly. Happily even." His mouth had one of those hidden smiles, and she groaned again at his smirk before closing the door on him.

She flopped onto the chair again, put her feet back up, and pulled her coffee to her chest, breathing it in for a long while before she took a sip. Rita had turned on the wireless while she was changing her dress and the sound of a low-wailing feminine voice filtered into the parlor. Violet dipped a butter biscuit into her coffee and enjoyed the sweet biscuit combined with the deep bitter coffee.

"Who would you prank?" Violet called to Rita.

Rita's voice was a little muffled as she answered, "Besides Ham?" She appeared in the doorway, straightening her dress.

Violet gaze sharpened and her mouth twisted evilly.

"Oh," Rita said.

"Oh," Violet agreed.

Their gazes met and a slow, smooth, snakish smile appeared on their faces in unison.

"We shouldn't," Rita tried.

Violet snorted and only just kept from lifting her brow. "Don't waste your breath, doll."

Rita's evil snicker echoed Violet's.

Vi adjusted her powder and lipstick, placed the cups on the tray, and then grabbed her handbag. It had her usual things. She always carried money, cards, a small book, a key to her house, Victor's house...and Ham's home. She had gone and gotten his dogs often enough to need one, and his neighbors were now used to her appearing randomly for the dogs.

"Should we short-sheet his bed?" Rita asked.

"Why wouldn't we?" Violet demanded.

"Maybe we could catch a snake."

"No," Violet shook her head. "It's far less funny when you see someone standing on a chair screaming."

Violet remembered it, but this time with the idea that everyone had been all right.

When she smirked and Rita snorted, Violet muttered, "Ginny is doomed."

She led the way out of the penthouse suite and they took the lift to the main floor where a uniformed porter ran to get them a black cab.

"Where should we go first?"

Vi looked at the cabbie. "Where would you go to buy items to prank a friend's home?"

He twisted in his seat and looked them over as if to check they were adults instead of children. After a moment he said, "A thrift shop since I'm guessing these things will be tossed in a bin by the poor bloke you're winding up."

Violet eyed Rita, who nodded to the man. After a rather longer amount of time than it took to reach most of the shops they usually visited, Rita and Violet found a shop stuffed full in every corner.

Rita gasped and turned in place. The boutique they visited the last time they went shopping had been set up like a ladies boudoir, with stockings arranged in a drawer and nighties tossed almost casually over a chair.

This place was a dusty mess. The part of Violet that tucked things away came clawing to the forefront. She felt almost as if her skin were crawling. Rita, however, dove right into the thick of it. She gasped again. "Look at this!"

A rusty saw? Violet shook her head and wandered, carefully not touching anything. Rita cackled as she found an old lipstick tube. She picked up several worn dolls with porcelain heads. One had a broken hand, one had been glued back together, and the last was in good shape, but somehow it was the creepiest of them all.

Was it the angle of the eyes? Or the curl of the hair? It was as though the doll was looking directly at you.

"That doll makes me feel as though she just might use the saw on me," Violet said with a grimace.

"Perfect," Rita said. She added odds and ends until her arms were overflowing while Violet attempted to avoid each brush of the place.

"What is your problem?" Rita asked.

"It's messy in here," Violet said low, knowing she was ridiculous.

"You wash," Rita scoffed.

"I know I'm being absurd," Violet admitted. "I just...don't like clutter."

Rita's scoff was enough to get Violet digging through a basket of things, and then her attention was caught by taxidermy. Slowly she walked closer. It was a squirrel that someone had dressed in a top hat and a coat. It was both horrible and fabulous. Ham needed it on his bedside table.

Rita grinned as Violet ignored the dust and the mess to purchase a taxidermy squirrel dressed for a night on the town.

CHAPTER 6

*G*inny stared between Violet and Victor and then placed a pamphlet before them.

"Autumn's Wind School?" Violet glanced at Victor, who lifted the pamphlet and read it quickly. Violet was far less concerned with the school itself as with Ginny. Her eyes were wide, she was biting her lip —she truly wanted to go to this school, Violet thought.

"They let you choose your classes and attend as you wish," Ginny told them.

Victor winced, but Violet asked, "Why does that appeal so much?"

"Because I hate chorus. And I'm brilliant at maths and I hate sitting through repetitive explanations for those who struggle. Why should I have to waste my time in that way? I like that you can pursue what interests you."

Violet saw the same truth in her twin's eyes that

was dwelling in hers. *They* couldn't have been trusted with that much freedom. The two of them would have disappeared into the green, the wood, whatever garden was there, and they'd have spent the day lying on a blanket, eating apples, playing fiction games, and avoiding all signs of actual work.

Together they faced Ginny. Victor asked, "How will you decide what to study?"

Ginny's hands were twisting in her lap. "I was hoping to...be a doctor?"

Violet blinked, staring at Ginny. There were, Vi was sure, women doctors. There could not, however, be very many. She didn't want to tell Ginny it couldn't be done. Vi had, in fact, little doubt Ginny would be brilliant at anything she decided to do.

"Why?" Violet asked.

"If my grandmother had someone looking after her in time she might have lived longer. My mother might not have died or my baby sister. My father might have lived longer too. I—" Ginny blinked rapidly and looked away.

"Then you shall be a doctor," Victor told her. "It won't be easy."

"You'll have to study harder than Victor and I ever did."

"I won't have to waste my time on chorus and painting, both of which I'm hopeless at, when I could be studying chemistry and anatomy."

"We'll have to visit the school before we decide," Violet told her.

Ginny nodded and then rose to pace. Violet watched the girl use Vi's own coping method.

"For better or worse," Victor murmured, "she's one of us."

Violet shrugged and then scowled when Victor lifted a brow at her to remind her that they were supposed to stop with their sarcastic gestures.

"Ginny, what is wrong?" Violet asked

She shook her head.

"You can tell us."

"It's just school stuff. A few of the girls . . . nothing to be worried about. I am just remembering how much I hate them."

"Yes, well—" Victor started to reply, paused to consider, and then added, "We all do, Gin."

Violet scoffed. "You stay here at Victor's, Ginny. The servants are off tonight."

Ginny absently nodded, and Vi rose with a slight motion of her head to her brother. He followed after her.

"Are we doing the wrong thing?" he asked.

"I have no idea."

"I feel like we should know."

"I suspect," Vi countered, "that none of them ever did. Not Aunt Agatha or Father or anyone. I think they were all just...just...faking it."

Victor muttered something dark and then admitted, "I have no idea what I'm doing with Ginny, Agatha, or Vivi. This is worse than not making enough money back when we were poor and had to scrape for cocktail money."

Violet grinned at him as she remembered those days. "Do you remember how bad our rooms smelled? It was constantly like old, wet socks."

Victor's laugh-snort had Vi giggling in response.

"Dancing, Victor. Cocktails. Possibly watching Rita and Ham fight."

Victor tugged one of Violet's locks, and she smacked him lightly before making her way through the garden back to her house. As she arrived, she found Hargreaves sending off the servants.

"How are you, Hargreaves? I hope you have good plans for the evening?"

He smiled and nodded. "The house is already locked up. All that you need to do is lock the front door, ma'am."

Violet nodded, skipping past him and down the hall as she called, "Have a good evening, Hargreaves."

Violet dressed quickly, choosing a black dress. It reached just above her knees with long fringe that fell beyond. The black beading was designed into the same black spider webs as her costume. Vi had liked the costume so much, she'd ordered one perfect for cock-tails and dancing.

Violet blended eyeshadow about her eyes, lined them with kohl, and applied mascara. She had already layered rouge and powder on her cheeks. She played with her new black diamond choker before putting it about her neck. Who, she wondered, would be pranking her house that night?

She was afraid that she'd come back to her house burned down. She turned to put on her shoes and found Jack sitting on the end of their bed watching her. She gasped.

"Make a noise next time, Jack. I was sitting here thinking about our house being burned down while we're gone, and then you're lurking."

"Lurking?"

"Like Frankenstein's monster."

He laughed. "How many spooky novels have you read in the last few weeks?"

"I don't know what you're talking about."

Jack crossed his arms over his chest.

"Fine." She scrunched up her nose and held up a finger for each title. "*Frankenstein. Dracula.* A large selection of Edgar Allan Poe's stories. *Carmilla. The Phantom of the Opera. The Picture of Dorian Gray.*"

"You might need to cut back on those."

"Do you *remember* someone putting mice through the letter slot? Or the snake in the library?"

Jack laughed, taking her hands and pulling her close to him so she was standing between his knees. "Are you afraid?"

"Who, me?"

"Yes," he said gently. "You. Do you want to go on a trip? Remove the chance for the prankster to bother us?"

Violet considered and then admitted, "No. I want to have our party, visit this odd school Ginny has picked out, and possibly lie on the library floor in front of the fire again, entirely unafraid of snakes."

"It is an excellent place to curl up with ginger wine and *Frankenstein.*"

"And maybe my husband."

"What a lucky man." Jack tugged her again, so she was forced to crawl onto his lap. While she was there she decided to place a kiss on his cheek. "So you aren't afraid?" he asked.

"Not at all. Irritated. I want to wring someone's neck."

He laughed. "Ham is looking into the people associated with our past cases. I had a thought, however."

Violet's head cocked.

"Do you think it could be your cousin, Algie?"

She nodded instantly. "Especially if Clara doesn't know. His wife might be happy to go along with pranks, but she'd probably draw the line at the snake. Algie is certainly dumb enough not to realize that an adder is poisonous."

"We need to look into Algie. And your brother, Geoffrey."

"Isn't he *still* down from school?"

Jack nodded. "As far as I can tell, London is full of students who've been sent down from school for poor behavior."

"My brother is an excellent choice." Violet sighed. "I want him to be less of a wart, but I can imagine Geoffrey having done this so easily."

Jack shook his head. "I told him I'd take him out tomorrow. We're going to a fight, and we're going have dinner at the Savoy."

"Romantic." Violet grinned at him and then laughed as Jack stood, holding her still, so she was floating in the air.

He snorted and then groaned as Vi eyed him. "We do have bad habits. It's possible we're irritating and poorly behaved."

Violet laughed, wrapping her arms around his neck.

"I used to be a respected investigator."

"Ohh," Violet whimpered for him and then made a kissy face. "Have you talked to Ham since you saw him at lunch?"

Jack's gaze narrowed on her. "Why would that matter?"

Her laugh was her only reply.

"He's coming tonight. He said he'd bring a spare shirt."

Jack carried her down the stairs as though she were a mud-covered toddler. When they reached the front of the house, they saw their vehicle had been brought around.

Jack opened the auto door and then paused. "Bloody hell," he groaned, sputtering out an expletive.

"Is that feces?" Vi stepped back, covering her face.

"I love my automobile, Vi!" he yelled as he slammed the door hard enough to rattle the window glass.

"I'm sure it can be cleaned." Her lips were pressed together to hold back the laugh of relief.

Victor and Kate approached and Violet crossed to her twin while Jack kicked the auto's wheels.

"What happened?" Victor asked.

"I'm guessing it is horse manure."

"Oh," Kate said, wincing. She tucked her arm through Victor's. "Why aren't you upset?"

"I'm relieved it wasn't the house on fire. I was thinking they were going to take it to that level."

"That's quite a bit beyond mice in the letter slot, pretty devil," Victor told her as Jack kicked the auto's wheels one more time.

Jack's smoothed-back hair was loose enough to flop down, and Violet nudged Victor. "You have a comb, don't you?"

"The smell may never come out," Jack growled. "When I find this bloke, I'm going to need to be disabled before I commit murder myself."

"I've got you, old man," Victor told him. "Come now. Let's get a black cab, a strong drink, and you can have a dose of dancing."

Jack glared at his auto and then muttered, "I'd like to have a dose of boxing."

"I'm all dressed up, Jack," Violet told her, "and I'm hungry. Disappear if you must, but Kate and I are going to have a roast beef, asparagus, and mushrooms."

Jack glanced at her and then back at the auto. "The servants are gone."

"They are."

"I don't want to clean it up myself."

"It's why we pay them." Violet winced as she looked at the auto. "They might need bonuses for the snake-mice-feces fiascos."

"Fine. Whatever. I want my auto back to normal. We're finding this bastard," Jack said, then he cleared his throat, striding ahead.

"He's angry," Kate said. "I hadn't realized he loved his auto so much."

"He startled me tonight," Violet said, speaking low. "I think he realized I am jumpy because of the pranks. He's too protective to have me wincing at *him* without growing furious."

Victor sighed and admitted, "That would have infuriated me as well."

Kate admitted in a low whisper to Violet. "The babies are sleeping in our rooms, just in case. We raised a couple of part-time servants to full-time until things are stopped. The dogs are in our room as well, so we're having something of a chaotic zoo."

"This needs to stop," Vi muttered. "This needs to stop before we're driven mad."

Jack was able to signal a black cab once they reached a busier street. Thankfully it wasn't raining and they were able to slide into the auto and head towards the restaurant.

"What do you think of Geoffrey for the prankster?" Jack asked Victor.

"I think Geoffrey likes you too well for that," Victor answered. "But he is dumb enough to think those things would be funny. Isn't he at school?"

"He got sent down about the same time as Ginny." Jack put his arm around Violet and she could feel the tension in him. "Seems there was a recent full moon and an excess of schools are without children after fights, pranks, shenanigans, and out-and-out crimes."

"I bet they just wanted to be home for All Hallows," Kate said. "It wouldn't be the first time school kids timed their hijinks to allow themselves to get out of school at the right time."

"Maybe there was also a big exam," Victor suggested. "I did that. Twice, actually."

Jack shook his head and glanced at Vi. "And you?"

"Victor and I generally timed our mischief to reach the same end."

"All Hallows at home," Victor said with a wicked grin. "Aunt Agatha always knew what we were up to and seemed to forgive us before we arrived."

CHAPTER 7

*H*am met them at the door of the restaurant. "Rita hasn't arrived yet." His gaze moved to Violet.

She grinned at him

"Do I need to ask for my key back?"

"Do you need someone to care for your dogs? Mary and Watson were happy to see me, and I took them for a good walk."

"You scared the boy I *pay* to walk my dogs."

Jack looked from one to the other as Violet and Ham bantered, and he finally asked, "What did you do?"

"It was mostly me," Rita said, appearing from behind them with Denny and Lila.

"Hullo, hullo," Denny said. "What did you do, Rita? And why didn't you tell us on the way?"

"I don't know to what you're referring," Rita immediately countered.

"So the message on the mirror was not from you?" Ham's gaze was fixed on Rita's face and she blushed deeply as they were led to their table. She muttered something low to Ham that the rest of them could not hear, but when Violet's interested gaze fell upon the couple, she didn't miss the way Ham had tangled his fingers with Rita's.

"What did you do?" Jack asked Violet again.

"Wiled away the afternoon," Violet suggested.

"I assumed you'd have gone shopping."

"We did," Rita said evilly. Her wicked cackle had everyone turning her way, and then she shrugged both innocently and entirely unconvincingly.

"Vi?" Victor asked. His gaze met hers and she met his gaze openly. Firstly, he could read her like a book. Secondly, he could never guess what they'd done. Therefore thirdly, despite his twin abilities, there was no reason to believe he could share anything Vi was hiding.

"They seemed to have dyed muslin with tea and shredded it. Simply bolts of it," Ham reported after ordering a stiff drink. "Artfully strung about my rooms as though some sort of cross between spiders and cobwebs had attacked my home."

Victor accepted his G&T and laughed.

"Violet, I believe, was responsible for a diorama of taxidermy next to my bed."

Vi simply sipped her drink, a Bee's Knees, and tried to convey the honeyed sweetness in her expression.

She didn't seem to be successful, but she clung to her efforts all the same.

"Rita, however," Ham continued, "left me a message in a rather disturbing shade of orange on my mirror. I'm not certain that the girl who cleans my rooms will be able to get it off with any accuracy. She also hid all my ties, short-sheeted my bed, and removed all of the wine, gin, whiskey, and bourbon from my rooms. I had to suffer the indignities of their wanton corruption without any solace. She left me a series of notes in my books, all of which had been turned spine inward."

"Why do you think that was me?" Rita demanded.

"Violet is much neater than you. If she'd turned them around, they'd have been rearranged into proper order and neatly lined on the shelves."

"Your shelves do give me hives," Violet said idly as she sipped her cocktail again, ignoring the shocked looks that were being sent her and Rita's way. As she met Jack's gaze, she told him, "Rita had a message to give Ham. I was merely an instrument in her delivery."

"So you bought him taxidermy."

"They gave the squirrel rather effeminate eyelashes. It couldn't be left to suffer in that dust shop."

"You took his bourbon?" Victor asked, aghast. "Vi!"

"I didn't," Violet countered. "I felt quite badly, so *I* left Ham a box of chocolates and a bottle of quite old scotch. Rita, however, said he'd have to suffer without my gift."

"Someone ate one bite of each chocolate."

"I was hungry," Rita lied. "Vi made quite a pig of herself with the petit fours."

Vi gasped, gaze narrowed on Rita, who refused to admit to her lie. "She thought it would be funny. I disagreed."

Denny shook his head. "I feel left out."

"They took my wine and bourbon," Ham told Denny flatly.

"I think I could survive long enough for a delivery."

"They ate my chocolate," Ham added.

At that, Denny shuddered. "You can strike our home with your mischief all the same. Lila's mother has decided to bring Martha to London, so just wait for them. I think...dare I say...Lila and I are going to flee. We're thinking Paris. I suspect if we stay anywhere nearby that her mother will use it as a prod and arguing point for the rest of our lives." He put on a high-pitched voice. *"Remember that time you abandoned us in London while you went to the Lake Country?* Every single Christmas. Every single family dinner. At every single request for every single future favor. A trip to the continent will look more planned."

Violet snorted and then groaned as every single person at their table turned on her. "I know! I know! We're supposed to be stopping."

Jack took mercy on Violet and told the others of what had happened to his auto. "What have you learned?" he asked Ham after his impassioned description.

"It's not great," Ham admitted. "Hugo Danvers escaped from his work detail about four weeks ago.

He was pretty far from London, so the locals haven't picked up the story, but he could be here by now."

"Where's Isolde?" Jack asked Violet. Both of them were immediately worried about Vi's sister who had once been kidnapped by the criminal. "Are they still at the country property?"

Violet shook her head. "They're in Brussels. My stepmother appeared, and they finally left their own house to get rid of her." Violet met Jack's gaze and then said, "I'm sure he does hate us."

"And Ginny is with us," Victor added. "If he knows that Ginny is here, he might add her into his revenge."

"Maybe we should send her away?" Violet asked and then shook her head and answered her own question. "I don't think we can do that. I am almost positive she's testing us to see if we *want* her around."

"I agree with that," Kate said.

"I need another drink." Victor lifted a finger for the waiter and ordered second drinks for all of them while they added their orders for dinner as well.

"I feel like needing another drink is the theme of this prankster," Violet said. "What is going to happen next? And will it finally end somehow being of greater damage than replacing parts of the auto or adding cats to the house?"

They ate with that glum thought hanging over them. They danced later and had cocktails and spun under the lights and things seemed brighter. Finally, Jack said, "Let's go home."

"Mmm," Violet agreed, laying her head on his arm. It must have been past two o'clock in the morning when she and Jack left the club. Victor and Kate had left long before, but they had to worry about their babies, given the prankster.

Violet snoozed against Jack's arm until they arrived at their house. Jack growled and Violet woke to the sound of his voice. "Something happened, Vi."

The house was not lit-up, which is what she would have expected if something had happened. But Hargreaves was standing with the local constable on the front step. Jack got out of the black cab and handed Violet out after him, paying the man while Violet slowly walked towards the house.

"I almost don't want to know. What if there's feces on our bed now?"

Jack shook his head and put his arm around her. "What happened, Hargreaves?"

"Someone broke the back window," he said, sounding as bothered as the rest of them. "Whoever it was broke every lightbulb in the house and left the furniture and beds strewn with glass. Small things were taken, but thankfully, I'd had the girls lock up the more expensive items earlier this morning. I'm afraid your manuscript was tossed on the fire, ma'am."

Violet gasped and to her surprise, tears filled her eyes. She had been *nearly* done. "Oh," was all she said. She glanced at Jack, at Hargreaves, and then muttered, "I'm going to my room at Victor's."

She left them all, but Jack followed quickly, walking her to the house, unlocking the door, and seeing her inside. Vi wanted nothing more than to open Victor's door and tell him she was there, but she couldn't risk waking the babies. Instead, she cracked the door and whispered, "Holmes?"

A moment later, both of her dogs appeared in the doorway, followed by a sleepy Victor. He took one look at Vi's face and went back for the basket of puppies as Violet made her way to her old bedroom. She hadn't slept in it since she'd married Jack, and she'd never expected to feel so sad when she stood in the doorway again.

Victor settled the puppies near the fireplace, lit the fire that had been laid, and left again without a word.

"Are you all right?" Jack asked.

Vi nodded, but it was a lie.

"I need to talk to Hargreaves and the constable. I'll be back soon."

She nodded, and it was fine. It wasn't so much that she was scared or hurt. She was *haunted.* Someone walked through her house. They'd taken something she'd worked on for weeks and destroyed it. They could have easily taken the pearls that Victor had bought her in Cuba or the long strand of creamy white pearls that Aunt Agatha had given her. They could have destroyed her small painting of Aunt Agatha on the vanity.

Violet pressed her lips together and changed into the nightgown that Victor brought. He took a seat in the chair near her fire while she disappeared into the bath to wash her face, clean her teeth, and change into the pajamas. He'd even brought her one of the kimonos she'd given Kate, which felt like home.

"They ruined the book," Violet told him, taking the

chair opposite him. His low curse illustrated her feelings as well.

"Anything else?"

"I don't know. They haven't been able to work the bottom part of the lightbulbs out. I guess they didn't take them out and crush them. They broke them still in the fixtures. Hargreaves had only been able to light lanterns. Plus it's too late to bring a man in to fix things or to clean it well."

"You're going to have to add me to the list of those who might commit murder, Vi. Are you going to have to replace everything? Maybe we should just flee to the country?"

Vi shrugged. She had no idea how it would all go. Would she throw herself on her bed a few weeks from now and have a random piece of missed glass cut her? Would their servants all quit, finding the aggravation not worth the pay? "We've invited all of our friends to the party at the museum, Victor."

"After," Victor suggested.

"After," Violet agreed.

Violet sighed as she looked towards the door of her bedroom. She knew that Jack was still dealing with whatever had happened and she knew he'd come before too much longer. She hadn't expected her house to feel quite so....violated. But that was the right word.

CHAPTER 8

$\mathcal{V}$iolet woke in her old room and frowned. Jack had left while Violet was still sleeping, placing a kiss on her forehead before disappearing. She took in a deep breath and then dug through her closet until she found an old dress. It was gray to match her mood, but she refused to succumb to the blue days just because some…some…*fiend* was messing with them.

Violet popped a bright pink jumper over the top of her gray dress, found her way to Kate's dressing room and put on a pretty pink rouge to give her face the flush of happiness, and then added some of Kate's pale pink lipstick. A little mascara and Violet felt as though she could face whatever had happened at her house.

Because she could, she took her dogs down to the garden and played with them—puppies included—until they were panting, curled up under the bushes, and then Violet took them inside just in case the criminal turned his or her attention to Victor's house.

She followed the path between Victor's house to her own and approached from behind. There was already a man at the window, removing the broken shards to add a new glass.

Violet watched for a while and then walked into her house. There was a small fleet of men working in the hallway. Two were on ladders dismantling the lighting fixtures while others were cleaning the floors. Hargreaves hadn't just brought in their servants, he seemed to have hired a whole army of additional servants.

Violet shook her head and slowly walked through the house. Two women were carrying an oriental rug out through the front door. Violet watched as they carried the rug out to the street where they could beat the glass off of the rugs and then sweep it up. There were a couple more servants out there already, beating another rug that she thought came from her office.

Jack's auto was gone from in front of the house, and Violet assumed that Hargreaves had taken care of that as well. Vi found her way to Beatrice's office. Vi's former maid was rearranging stacks of papers by the light of the open window.

"Here too?" Vi asked.

Beatrice gasped as she grabbed her chest. "Oh!"

"I'm sorry," Vi laughed. "I'm jumpy too. I'm just surprised whoever this is went after you too."

"I think they were just spreading mischief," Beatrice admitted. "Mostly my papers were shuffled and all the lights were affected."

Violet sighed as she glanced around. She could see that there just weren't enough brooms to go around and Beatrice hadn't been able to sweep up the glass in her office. The crunch, crunch of it would probably scratch the floors, Vi thought, and they'd be refinishing them shortly even though they had just before they moved into the house.

Violet smiled at Beatrice, inquired after her family, and left the maid to sort out her regular letters from the party organizing and from the reports on the orphanage that Violet and Victor supported.

Violet hurried towards Jack's office and found him watching as one of the men in overalls used pliers to remove the remains of the last lightbulb.

"We've got the electricity turned off," the man said, "so we can't test it quite yet, but you should be sorted out."

The maids had already worked in Jack's office. All signs of crushed glass were gone.

"They used our china too," Jack told Violet. She winced and then muttered, "All of it? Even Aunt Agatha's?"

He frowned as he nodded and Violet had to fight another flood of tears. She was going to commit murder, she thought. She was going to find this fiend, take them captive, torture them, destroy the things they loved, and then smother them to death.

Rather than cry, Violet fisted her hands.

"Perhaps we should call off the party," Jack suggested.

Violet shook her head. She'd be...well, she'd be *damned* if this person drove Violet into admitting defeat. "We've already paid for it all, Jack. What else can they do? No. We're having the party and we're setting a trap."

"Agreed," Jack said. "I've already talked to John Smith. That man is sneaky enough to catch anyone. He's going to be lurking and seeing what he can find. Perhaps we have an unknown enemy."

Violet shook her head, wondering what they could have *possibly* done to deserve this. She pretended to smile and kissed Jack's cheek, but she knew he didn't believe her lie of a grin any more than she believed his.

"It'll be all right, Vi darling."

How could they say such a thing? They were blind-sided with each attack even when they thought they'd prepared. Who'd have imagined that someone would be bold enough to dump manure in Jack's auto and get away with it?

"The constable will be back this morning with another man from Scotland Yard," Jack told her. "I called Ham even though this is a little petty of a crime for what he normally does. It turns out his superiors minded less when he emphasized who your father was."

"Ah, the good earl," Violet muttered and then winked when Jack examined her too closely. Vi both hated the special treatment her father could invoke for her and used it often enough to know she was a bit of a hypocrite.

She left him, clinging to the lie of happiness as she made her way to her own office. If there was a particular viciousness aimed at their house, it was here. Her typewriter had been flung over. The maid had righted it, but Violet could see that it would need to be repaired. A new girl was working in the corner. She had a soft look about her as she swept the floors and she was doing quite a poor job of it.

"Would you leave, please," Violet told her. "Send my secretary Beatrice to me."

Once the girl left, Violet took the broom she'd been using so poorly and swept. Removing the glass helped more than just watching. She watched the bristles of the broom scoop up the shards of glass and made quite a pile of it, noting the blue painted china amid the destroyed lightbulb.

There was something soothing in taking her office back, but when she'd dusted her bookshelves, removed the glass, and cleaned her desk, Beatrice still hadn't arrived.

Violet rang the bell and found that Hargreaves himself had answered it.

"What happened to the girl I put in here?" His eyes glinted with anger and Violet shushed him.

"It's fine," Vi said, "though, I did send the girl for Beatrice and was hoping someone could send her along. As for the room, I suppose that cleaning it myself makes me feel like I'm taking it back from whoever did this to us."

"They've nearly repaired all the fixtures, ma'am," Hargreaves said. "We'll be turning on the electricity again shortly to see if anything was permanently broken."

Vi nodded and then faced Hargreaves. "Are we going to lose anyone over this?"

Hargreaves shook his head. "Bringing in the extra help and offering bonuses helps. It also helps that you're good to them. They hear the horror stories from their peers, ma'am."

Violet shook her head, but she wasn't surprised. She was of the opinion that if you always treated the staff well, they were less likely to tell other people your secrets. She was certain that they knew at least most of the things she wouldn't announce in a newsletter.

Violet pressed her forehead and took a seat, hopping back up. The glass hadn't been swept from her chair, but her skirt was thick enough to prevent cuts. She shook her dress out as Hargreaves used a dust rag to wipe her chair thoroughly.

"Are you all right?"

She nodded and then leaned back. "Just send Beatrice, would you? Also, order a new typewriter and send this one to be repaired."

Hargreaves disappeared as Violet started working through her desk. Her manuscript had been destroyed, but there was also her letters and things that had been rifled through. Violet left her office and went to her bedroom. It had been thoroughly cleaned. Any sign of what had been done there had been removed. She heard a loud snap and then the overhead light turned on.

Violet saw a large black cat sitting in the corner of her room, and she hoped that it hadn't been hurt after the last day. She hadn't even considered the poor things.

Beatrice appeared a few minutes later and Violet said, "I need to focus on the party."

"Of course."

"Are things in order?"

"I haven't found everything yet," Beatrice said, "but I had worked through my to-do list yesterday, so it should all be fine."

Violet nodded. "Well, do what you can then for Hargreaves and do me a favor and contact my man of business, Mr. Fredericks. Have we upset anyone recently with our investments or lack thereof?"

"Perhaps, he might have some good ideas, but I don't think there was anything."

Violet sighed. "It doesn't make sense that this is happening. And whoever is doing it is a right fool. Ham and Jack can pull in constables."

Jack appeared in the door as if he'd known that they'd been speaking of him. "Smith has already found a lead."

Vi looked up.

"Someone put an advertisement in the newspaper, Vi. For pranks to be executed at a fee."

Vi stared.

"He's seeing what he can discover at the newspaper office and will be back."

Beatrice started to speak and then snapped her mouth closed.

"Speak," Violet told her one-time maid.

"That doesn't quite make sense," Beatrice said. "It might be connected, but whoever is engineering this must know something about your life. They were able to judge when you ordered your auto or when you'd be home for the mice or when the servants' evening off occurred."

Jack nodded and Violet groaned. There weren't many places that had all of those things written down. Especially—Violet shook her head and crossed to the table next to her bed, pulling it open.

She sat down, closing her eyes. Her journal was missing. Jack and Beatrice had both seen her open the drawer next to her bed enough times to understand the sick expression.

"Oh, my lady," Beatrice said softly.

"Vi, I swear, I will choke the life from this fiend, myself."

"It doesn't make any sense," Vi said. "The only person I've truly angered lately is Mrs. Partridge, but —I can't imagine..."

"We'll investigate. I'll set Smith on her."

"I told her I'd sell her back her part of the school," Violet said. "She can go on torturing girls. I'm not going to just donate the money, but asking for a return is reasonable."

Vi bit down on her bottom lip. She had written so many of her thoughts in her journal. It was in her writing that *she* discovered her thoughts. She had written about Jack and wishing that he'd stop working for Scotland Yard. She had written about loving Jack but missing her life with Victor before they'd married.

She'd written about being uncertain about becoming a mother. She'd written about her concerns over Ginny. Vi had written about her frustration with Lady Eleanor and how it still hurt that Vi was never good enough for her stepmother. She'd written about business thoughts and her concerns with an auto company she had invested in. Every piece of her life had been written starkly in her journal without a single concern that anyone would read it but herself.

She'd written out her struggles with her blue days and her notes on how she had been fighting them. She *needed* that information. It had guided what she decided to do on every side.

That journal was a guide to Vi's life. She was sick, painfully nauseous at the realization that this person who clearly despised Vi knew all of her private feelings. What would a person who would leave a poisonous snake in your house and destroy property so wantonly do with Vi's thoughts? What it was—it wouldn't be good.

CHAPTER 9

*V*iolet wasn't sure if the universe was looking after her when the day of All Hallows dawned without incident. Her perspective that edged too often towards the bleak seemed to declare that she was being dim. There wasn't some benign god that had stepped in to save Vi from further aggravation.

If there were, in fact, a fairness-balancing god, Violet knew she had been too blessed. Born to an earl? Vi's thoughts continued to wander as she dropped a black silk slip edged in lace over her head. Her ancestors had used the idea of some sort of "chosen by God to rule" to justify their great wealth and excess while everyone else suffered. It felt as though generations of karma deserved to land on Vi.

Times had changed, Violet thought. The reality was that Vi had been born to an earl and Beatrice to a small farmer. They were, both of them, simple human women. The differences in their statuses were nothing more than luck.

If anything, Violet thought, her true luck had been in her associations. A twin to a brother such as Victor, being raised by Aunt Agatha, falling in love with Jack.

"You're thinking too hard," Jack told her.

Violet considered him and then turned to her costume. It was a cross between a traditional witch's dress with short sleeves and a long skirt, adorned by a classic pointed hat and a typical evening dress for Violet with embroidery, beading, and being perfectly fitted to Vi's form. It gathered about her waist rather than giving a long, straight line like most of her dresses.

However, the fabric was embroidered with spider webs and sparkling black beads. She'd added her slew of new jewelry. She'd wound chunks of her hair into spiky little knots and held them in place with her new hairpins. She put the new choker about her neck, added her gold bangles and the new bracelets and her wedding ring on her finger and her spider ring on her opposite forefinger. Vi rang the bell for a maid to come and put her things away.

They were being careful now, with all their small valuables locked up when they weren't being used, including Violet's new manuscript.

Vi started with her cosmetics. She left off all rouge and added a heavy layer of powder so she was sickly pale. Then, she drew a large mole on her cheek quite near her lips. When she was satisfied with the mole, she added dark shadows around her eyes so they seemed to fade into darkness. The final touch was her lipstick. Unlike her usual red or pink lipstick, Violet had bought a berry color so dark, it was *almost* black.

When she was finished, she turned to Jack and spun in a circle. The boring man that he was, he wore only a very handsome suit with a domino mask. His eyes glinted with appreciation and humor, and he asked, "Is this the frivolous purchase?"

Vi grinned. If only the purchase of the sword had been as economical as her spider hairpins.

"They do look expensive, but I suspected something like jewelry. I suppose it makes this piece irrelevant." Jack handed Violet a slim velvet case, and she gasped.

"Speaking of being frivolous creatures."

It could have been made to match her spider hairpins and ring. A string of black gemstone spiders, one after another, that would wrap around her wrist to look as though they were climbing her arm. She quickly removed her bangles and tossed them back into the jewelry box, so her diamond and ruby bracelets were on one wrist and the spider cuff was on the other.

"I love it!" Violet jumped into his arms and pressed a very dark kiss to his face.

He groaned while she wriggled to be let down to reapply her lipstick, then put it into a black clutch that was embroidered with white and red silk spiders.

There was a knock at the bedroom door and Jack

answered it, wiping her lipstick from his face. "Victor?"

"I—"

It was all Violet needed to know that something was amiss. She closed her eyes and breathed slowly in before she faced him.

His gaze met hers with the extensive worry she knew from her blue days, from when they'd realized Aunt Agatha was really gone, and from the early days when they'd been scraping by in their smelly rooms and something came up.

"Is it the babies?"

He shook his head.

"Kate?"

Another negative.

"Ginny? The dogs?"

Before Victor could shake his head again, Jack snapped, "Tell us."

"Someone cut out the parts of your journal that pertained to me and delivered them through my letter slot."

Vi froze. Her throat was thick. She was *sick* at the thought. Her gaze searched his frantically and he said, "I *know* you, Vi. Don't worry."

Her eyes welled with tears and her nose burned, but she bit down on the inside of her cheek with fierce determination not to cry.

"I miss you too," he said gently.

Violet crossed to him and wrapped her arms around his waist, pressing her head into his chest. He was the rock of her entire life, and if she had hurt him while she worked out her own feelings, she'd carry it for too long.

"There was another one," Victor told her. "It was on the table in your hall. I took it when I came up the stairs."

"It's for Jack," Vi guessed.

"There was one for Ginny too."

Violet's mind raced as she wondered what she could have said that would have been worth revealing about Ginny. She took that one from Victor and read it frantically.

Ginny is home again. I find myself staring at her and thinking, my God, what am I supposed to do with her?

The next piece hadn't actually been written about Ginny, but Violet swallowed with horror as she read it.

...yet again, we're facing problems with her. I've told Jack we should get rid of her, but he seems to think we can find a good place for her. My only requirement is that it's far from here.

Violet sat down with horror and held her hand out for the ones she'd written about Victor. He handed it over without a word, and she read it through. It was mostly true. She did miss him. She did want her old life back at times. Just in passing whimsies. Not really. Most of it came from her grieving for Aunt Agatha. Vi wanted the past Christmases at Aunt Agatha's with too much sherry and the same treats that Cook had made.

"I didn't say that stuff about Kate," Violet told him, handing it back, but he refused to take her chopped up journal pages.

"When you refer to the tilt of a nose, Vi, it's always in reference to Lady Eleanor. I had little doubt."

Violet handed him the bit for Ginny. "The sending her away was about the mean horse who bit."

Violet had let Jack have the pieces that had been written about him. Instead of opening it, he'd watched her with concerned eyes.

"Aren't you going to read the horrible things I said about you?"

"Violet," Jack said gently. "I know you love me. I love you. I don't need to read some chopped-up version about how you think I'm too protective."

"You are."

"Or that you miss the simplicity of your life when it was you and Victor and there wasn't a fortune to handle and all the rest of this. Do you think I don't miss the simpler days too?"

Violet stared.

"You're a handful, Vi."

With a watery laugh, she said, "You're no Prince Charming."

"Agreed." Despite the presence of Victor, Jack leaned down, cupped Violet's cheeks, and kissed her breathless. Somewhere in the process, Victor disappeared and Violet found a willingness to have a good evening.

"Ginny didn't see her devilish note," Vi told him as she reapplied her lipstick yet again. "Victor knows me too well to be bothered, and you already know my flaws. This wasn't so bad, I guess."

The two of them met the other's gaze and in unison, they winced.

"It feels like the axe is about to fall," Jack said. "There are guard dogs at our house to go with the cats. We haven't seen a mouse in days. The constables have triple staffed both here and at the party. That fiend investigator, John Smith, is on the case."

Violet followed Jack down the stairs. Everyone she knew and loved in London or reasonably close would be in attendance at the party. They had ordered black cabs since Jack's auto was still being fixed and Victor wanted to avoid the same fate.

The black cabs were waiting and Violet glanced back at Hargreaves.

"Did Beatrice already go?"

He shrugged a little helplessly. "She didn't tell me she was going to, but she's not in her rooms."

Violet's brows lifted and then she grinned at him. "Just get her another black cab if she appears. I'm sure she's working. She always is."

Hargreaves dared to grin as he replied, "I think she learned it from you, ma'am."

Violet let Jack seat her in the auto and asked Kate, "How are my babies?"

"They're teething," Kate groaned. "I've already had two aspirin and a cocktail. I couldn't love them more, but I'm not sure we haven't made a terrible mistake."

Violet curled her arm around Jack's but refrained from pressing her face to him. She had layered quite a lot of powder on her face. It might be better to curl into his arms, risking his fine black suit, *after* the party.

"Did anyone see who left the notes?" Jack asked Victor.

Vi's twin shook his head and then muttered, "We hadn't thought to have someone looking. We got the guard dogs like you said. We changed our locks when you changed yours. We've even barred the nursery windows, though we'll be removing the bars after this is over. My goodness, there's a maid whose job it is to stay with the dogs so we don't lose one. This feels like we should just flee south."

"We are fleeing south," Kate told Victor. "The moment we convince Vi to go."

Vi nodded. "Let's go all the way to the Amalfi coast. It would be good for all of us."

"It has been too long," Victor said. "We could get Isolde to go. We haven't even seen the baby yet."

"Who knew that being the favored child was so much worse than being the unwanted stepchildren?" Vi's mean laugh was echoed by Victor. Their stepmother had always despised the two of them while vastly preferring her own children.

It was just that Isolde had become her own person and didn't share her mother's views. Of the twins, of parenting, of money, and of status.

"You wrote to Tomas about Danvers?" Jack asked Victor.

"And I sent a wire," Victor said. "Tomas replied saying they were going to catch a random ship to somewhere else and he'd be in touch."

"That's fun!" Violet murmured.

Everyone looked at her, and she said, "Well *not* fleeing, but just picking a place based upon the first ship available. Letting chance be your guide."

"What if it was going to Africa?"

"I'd like to see lions." Vi glanced at all of them and then added, "Rita loves Africa."

"She's spent too much time with Rita," Victor told Jack. "As the husband, it's your responsibility to nip that before we're getting postcards from Timbuktu."

CHAPTER 10

The museum was lined with carved turnips. They were lit and horrifying. Wrought iron candlesticks that reached waist high stood on each step up the walk, giving a spooky, flickering light. A servant was at the base of the walk, reviewing invitations, while another was at the top of the walk, doing the same. Violet noted the constable in the shadows of the front door and knew that inside there was another wearing a domino and cape while a third was at the back of the museum near the garden.

Violet placed her own spider mask on her face. She'd given her spookier mask to Beatrice because the maid wanted to monitor the party unobserved. Vi placed her hand on Jack's elbow and walked up the steps with him, meeting Victor and Kate at the top of the steps.

Victor was dressed as a pirate, something she

hadn't even noticed in her earlier distress. Kate was wearing a gown embroidered with tentacles and she held a small trident in her hand and a tiara of shells in her hair.

"You look lovely," Violet declared, walking in a circle around her friend.

Someone took Violet's hand and spun her, lifting her into the air and laughing hard. "Violet, you minx," Denny said, "I am *indeed* an idiot and a fool whose laziness led to escalating everything in Felixstowe."

Violet stared at him, realizing that more of her journal had been sent out.

"I love you too!" He pressed a kiss to either cheek and then added, "Let's catch this fellow. It's time to pull out the chalkboards and do stuff."

"Stuff?" Lila asked lazily. Her gaze met Violet's. "I didn't rate a mean letter from your tormentor, but I don't disagree with your assessment of Denny. He might have been offended if you, Jack, Victor, and I hadn't said it all to his face already."

"I did too," Ham announced as he joined them. He was wearing a domino mask, but it didn't do much to disguise him as his beard still gave him away.

"You would have had to shave," Violet told him, "for the mask to be successful."

"Oh, that wouldn't help," Ham muttered.

"Whyever not?" Denny demanded. "I've only just realized that none of us have seen your shorn mug. Are you horrible under your hair?"

"Rather," Ham said and then kissed Violet on the cheek. "I got one too, Vi. Not to worry."

Violet stared at him and then said low, "I don't know what I wrote, but she's—he's—whoever—is mixing in words that don't apply to the subject."

"Yes, that was rather obvious. It's also obvious to me that you reveal your thoughts through your writing, Vi. Those first passages rarely match the latter ones you know. It's why you write things out on the chalkboards when you're meddling. Your mind needs to see the words. I've a detective or two who are the same. To tell you the truth, they've taken to using chalkboards since I've realized."

Denny gasped and then tucked his arm through Vi's. "Vi! Our method is famous."

"Vi's method," Lila corrected.

Denny was dressed like a dog while Lila looked a princess.

"You've an interesting costume, my friend," Violet told him. She wasn't all that surprised to see Ham in his constable uniform, but she was rather shocked to see Rita leave the ladies and approach. She was Artemis, goddess of the hunt. With a slinky dress made of fine kid leather that dipped low at her generous chest and was torn high on her legs, she looked as though she were a man's wild dream come true. She had a quiver of arrows over her back and a bow that was placed diagonally over her body. Her sandals were tied around her calves, and her cosmetics were just shadowy and messy enough to seem both deliberate and wild.

"We can't all be glamorous like Rita," Denny announced, "and I am in the doghouse."

Violet kissed Rita's cheek as her stepmother crossed to greet them. "You should have been timely."

"We had a bit of trouble," Violet told Lady Eleanor. "I hope you've enjoyed yourself so far?"

"Not really. Your note was quite unkind."

Violet's fingers dug into Jack's arm as she replied, "My journal was stolen, Lady Eleanor. Pieces of it were mixed with other things I wrote to send horrible thoughts to people who were featured."

"A lady shouldn't have her thoughts bandied about."

"I agree," Violet told Lady Eleanor simply. "I'm sorry you were drawn into this trouble."

"You weren't easy, you know. You and Victor. You wanted your aunt, hated me, your father was of no help. None whatsoever. I don't know why I'm always the villain. I did my best!" The shrill voice of Lady Eleanor carried across the ballroom and Violet winced further as masked faces turned their way.

"Dance, why don't you?"

"You know I don't like to dance."

"Have a drink."

"The first I had was quite sour." Lady Eleanor screwed up her face as she added, "Usually, you can be counted on not to be serving garbage, but I see even that point of pride in you had to be ripped away."

Violet thought it was possible that she should have certainly lived a terrible previous life to have led her to this point. She glanced at Victor and said, "Victor will make you a drink. You know he's so talented."

Lady Eleanor started to scold, but to Vi's endless

shock, her stepmother pressed a handkerchief to her eye. "I just...I just...you were hardly easy." Her stepmother walked away, carrying herself with her usual stiff decorum.

Violet thought that an actual tear might have rolled down her stepmother's face. She looked up at Jack's masked face, which was hard to read on the best of days and asked, "Should we be nicer to her?"

He hesitated. "I think that kindness might always be the right choice, but she's hardly a victim, Vi."

Violet shook her head and then adjusted her mask. "Let's dance before my father scolds me for calling her Lady Eleanor and making her cry."

Jack pulled Violet onto the dance floor, and the band in the corner wailed out a jazz song full of heat. Jack's hand on her waist and the press of his chest against her body were enough to block out the world. Especially when his shoulders were broad enough to carry all her worries too.

She knew he felt as helpless as she did, entrenched in this guerrilla warfare with a fiend who didn't balk at concepts like consequences and morals. Forget those worries, Violet, she told herself.

The latest trick of the fiend hadn't been enough to ruin Vi's friendships, so perhaps she had one in her scorecard of losses.

"Your dance card is mine tonight," Jack told her. He lifted her hand and placed a kiss on her wrist just below where her spider cuff ended. She shivered in his arms and then heard her brother clear his throat.

"Are you trying to steal my partner when your own looks like a sea goddess come to life?"

"Someone ruined the alcohol. I've sent out to my regulars, but Vi, I don't think they'll be there. I also sent one of Ham's men to my house to drain the cellars."

"What do you mean?"

"It tastes like vinegar."

Vi frowned. "Were the bottles switched or tampered with?"

"Vi, I know my brands," Victor said. "Someone certainly tampered with the bottles and that's assuming you don't take into account the very clearly tampered stoppers. Are they all vinegar or just a few? Can we trust the ones that aren't off that something else wasn't put in there? Because this is the fellow who let a poisonous snake in your library."

Violet groaned. "Send someone to the nearest pub and buy whatever they'll sell. Pay top dollars. It just might be an evening for a hearty pint. Have you seen Beatrice?"

Victor shook his head and said, "Kate and I will see what we can do. I did see Gerald, and I'll send him the other way. We should be able to have beer and cider here before too much time passes."

Violet's father approached. "Oh, I see you've realized. I sent my man for some of my bourbon and wine. What is happening, Vi?"

She shook her head helplessly and then found her attention pulled once again by her cousin, Algie.

"Vi! Got your letter. Kind of mean, yes?"

"It was clearly not from her," his wife, Clara, said.

"But it was her writing. I told you I know my cousin's writing. She's called me a nincompoop to my face for years. I shouldn't see why it wasn't her this time."

Violet groaned and Denny called merrily, "Don't take it personally, old man. Got one of those myself." He pulled a flask from his inside pocket and said, "The key here, old boy, is to remember that you knew Vi could be a sour old puss before you got the letter and then you just shake it off and have a nip."

Algie laughed, seemingly unbothered, and took Denny's flask. "Don't mind if I do. Vi, the drinks tonight are garbage. Utter trash. I'm surprised Victor isn't rolling over in his grave."

"It's an All Hallows stunt someone played on poor Vi, you idiot," the earl told his nephew. "Victor's gone for beer and cider."

"The good cider?" Algie demanded.

"This is Victor we're talking about," the earl said. "Get to work, Jack. See what can be done."

Jack nodded and pressed a kiss on Vi's forehead. "Stay with Rita or Lila. Just in case this is more than vicious schoolboy pranks."

"They're not leaving in a rage," Violet told Rita as she took in her guests.

"You're the daughter of an earl, and the *earl* has announced loudly a good half-dozen times that when he finds the fiend playing All Hallows pranks on the cocktails, he'll have the man strung up."

"How did I miss that?" Violet asked, staring in shock at Rita.

"I suspect it was that dance between you and Jack. To be honest," Rita said with a low chuckle, waving her face, "I was a bit distracted myself and I was only catching glimpses."

Violet stared in horror, glancing up and noting that the lights were rather brighter than she'd intended. She closed her eyes and Rita laughed merrily. "She blushes!"

"She's a prude under all that jewelry," Lila told Rita in an aside. "She waited until her wedding day, did you know?"

Rita glanced at Vi and then back at Lila. "And you?"

"The key is understanding your natural rhythms and using the devices that are illegal and expensive."

Rita lifted a brow and then said, "Agreed."

Lila laughed at Rita's subtle confession.

"Do you think Ham will care?" Rita asked with a trace of worry.

"Do you think Ham is as pure as a little lamb?" Lila countered.

"I think men have different standards for women, and he doesn't…pressure me. Maybe he assumes—"

"Just tell him," Violet told Rita. "But not where Denny can overhear. He is both an idiot and a loudmouth."

"He is," Lila said fondly. "Nincompoop is accurate for both of those fools."

Violet followed Lila's gaze and found Denny and

Algie in the center of the dance floor, boisterously waltzing off-time.

"How do you stand it?" Rita asked Lila. "I like Denny, but he's a bit much."

"He makes me laugh," Lila told Rita simply, smiling fondly.

"He makes all of us laugh, but don't you get…tired of him?"

Lila shook her head. "I like to laugh. He *does* have a more serious side. It's just the part of him that is like a night-blooming flower. It only comes out with the right circumstances, but underneath all of his ridiculousness is a man that is as loving as Jack, as thoughtful as Victor, and quite frankly, a bit softer than Ham. We can't be serious all the time, Rita darling."

"Ham is a wolf," Violet agreed. "Almost always on the hunt."

"Or a beast," Rita sighed. "I suppose a daft duck like Denny would be easier than Ham."

"He would be," Lila said. "You are missing the essential difference. I am a lazy woman and I enjoy not having to constantly fight. I want Denny to be happy. He wants me to be happy. We'd both rather make the other happy than fight. It's peaceful. You'll battle Ham for every inch of your freedom. The only reason Violet doesn't have to is that Jack knows it's useless and Vi lingers in her moods. It leaves the man an anxious mess."

Rita met Violet's gaze and the two of them slowly turned back to stare at Lila.

"What? Just because I like to nap doesn't mean I'm stupid."

"I haven't told Ham yes, yet."

Lila rolled her eyes as she snorted. "It's just a matter of time, and don't harass me about snorting, rolling my eyes, lifting my eyebrow or sniffing dramatically."

CHAPTER 11

"We should have the nibbles put out," Violet said. "There are trays of toffee apples, chocolates from Mariposa's, and shrimp pots. Other usuals with some fanciful bites."

Violet glanced at the clock, noted the time, and realized that the scavenger hunt Beatrice was supposed to start was twenty minutes past due. Where *was* her secretary? Violet's concern grew when her mind flicked over the last time she'd seen the woman. It had been that morning while they went over the plan for the evening. Surely Beatrice would have checked in at some point? There had been no sign of her being at the party, no sign of that hideous mask, her maid's slender form, or the organization that flowed in her wake.

Violet hurried through the crowd until she found Ham. "Beatrice!"

His gaze narrowed on hers, hearing the worry. "I was wondering where she was."

"I haven't seen her all day. Not since before breakfast," Violet told him. "I'm so worried."

"I'll send one of the boys to track her down."

"Do you think they hurt her?"

Ham paused long enough to give Violet real terror, but his head shook. "No, Vi. I don't think we're dealing with a killer."

Violet nodded and then asked, "Should I start the scavenger hunt?"

"Do," Ham said. "She'll be all right, Vi."

Violet wished his words could give her more comfort. They had all faced the vagaries and monstrosities of mankind too often to ever feel all that safe.

Violet joined the band on the stage and then handed over the first clue and the rules. She couldn't do it. Or perhaps better said, she didn't want to. She left the songstress in charge and stepped back. The crowd was thick. It didn't seem that the bad cocktails had stopped anyone from being merry.

When the announcements were made, a rousing cheer went up despite the lack of alcohol. Violet noted the waiters with the trays starting amid the crowd and flicked over the masked faces, looking for those she knew.

Jack was there, near the wall, talking to Ham. Jack's gaze found hers, and she could feel the warmth of it on her. Kate had found Ginny and Geoffrey, and like the saint she was, Kate was chatting with the both of them. Ginny's spider costume was as fabulous as the girl herself. Near them was another woman with a half-mask, but Vi recognized that tell-tale smirk and the turn of the woman's mouth. Miss Allen had found Vi's ward.

What would happen next? Vi felt pressure starting to grow behind her eyes as a stressful headache mounted. Lila and Denny, Algie and his wife, Kate, Rita with Gerald, the earl, and Lady Eleanor. Those Vi loved most were safe at the moment. Now to find Beatrice. Violet turned to exit the stage as the crowd broke into their groups to retrieve the first clue. They were being sent on different routes through the clues to end in the garden where there would be a bonfire, and if anything of this entire evening came out all right, there would be flaming cocktails.

Victor had taught the staff they'd hired to make some American drink called *The Café Brulot Diabolique*. Violet had heard the description and been instantly sold on the creation. Coffee, brandy, citrus, and spices? Yes, Violet had replied when he'd told her of it. He had refused to make her one in advance, and she'd been looking forward to it before things had started to go awry.

Vi took the steps down off the makeshift stage, being handed down by one of the band members, when her gaze was caught by none other than Beatrice's mask! Vi gasped and raced towards Beatrice, but she was looking the other way.

Vi took the side door out of the ballroom and

raced down the hallway, chasing after the phantom of Beatrice who was moving quickly.

"Beatrice!" Violet called.

She looked back and then sped up.

"Beatrice!" Violet called again, even though she knew it wasn't her secretary. "Stop! Stop you!"

This portion of the museum was empty since the scavenger hunt led the visitors through the displays. It would end at the newest exhibition in the once-closed Transylvania room where the latest acquisition of the museum was mounted with a plaque from the donator.

Violet chased the form down the backstairs towards the kitchens, but when they'd have turned into the busy epicenter where waiters were gathering with their trays, the form darted out a back door and then disappeared.

Violet studied the garden, looking for a form, but it was gone. She'd have followed further, but she hadn't entirely lost her mind. There was a very distasteful replica of a guillotine in the back garden along with an iron maiden from torturing the poor women accused of being witches.

It was, in fact, a garden with a maze full of torture devices that had been gathered and placed among roses by the very odd owner of this establishment. Perfect for All Hallows, Violet had thought. How wrong she'd been!

Vi turned to go back inside, but her gaze was caught by two doors set into the back of the house, near the ground. Cellar doors! Was it possible that Vi had discovered the way this fiend had been accessing the party?

"Constable?" Violet called. "Constable?"

No one answered her and Vi shivered. Perhaps the constable had seen the fleeing figure and tracked them down, but she couldn't help but think the cruelty of this prankster had been increasing. If she'd been plagued by demons, Violet wouldn't have expected very much different from them as she was experiencing at the moment.

Violet hurried back inside and rushed into the kitchens to find someone to go check the cellars with her when she heard the shouting of the chef they'd hired.

"What is this madness?"

Violet stepped inside and found what looked to be a flock of waiters cowering away from the massive man in the center of the kitchen. "They are saying they are bad? They are not bad! They are—"

The man took one of the small bites Violet had ordered and popped it into his mouth. He spat it out and then turned on the assistant chefs. "What is this? Bad lobster? Who let the lobster spoil?"

They shook their heads.

The large man forced his way across the kitchens and stuck his hand in a small bowl, sniffing what he pulled out. "Sugar in the salt bowl! Bad fish! What manner of devilry is this?"

Violet closed her eyes.

"Sir?" The man who dared to speak squeaked a little when the massive chef rounded on him. "The toffee apples we ordered are onions."

The chef shrieked. Violet wanted to beg an aspirin, but she didn't trust anything from the kitchens.

"Enough," Violet snapped and the whole of the room faced her. "You," Violet said to the bravest of the men. "Go to whatever pubs you can find and bring in as much fish and chips as you can."

"Fish! Cod! Chips! I am an artist," the chef squawked. "An artist!"

"Enough," Violet snapped again, shouldering the persona of Lady Eleanor. "We have been tricked, my good friend. Are we going to let them win?"

He gasped. His gaze narrowed. "I am an artist."

"Then you can make the hearty, wholesome food your *most trusted* men are to acquire magical."

"I can't turn stone into gold, madam. Lady Violet will never hire me again. Never!"

"She will," Violet told him. "*I* will. I'm Lady Vi. Now calm down and get to it. Show me what dreams can be made of beer-battered cod and chips."

A furious gaze came into his eyes and he nodded frantically. "What you said—my most trusted men—do you think I have a cuckoo in my nest, my lady?"

"One of us does," Violet told him flatly.

He screeched again and three men were summarily sent away. As he shouted names of men and pubs, Violet hurried out of the kitchens.

"Vi! Don't run off like that!"

Vi found Jack and Victor staring her down.

She winced at the sick worry in their expressions before she explained. "I saw them! But I thought it was Beatrice. Once I realized, they were gone. Jack, the constable in the back garden isn't there, and I chased the fiend outside and there are cellars doors and I think I may have found the way in."

Jack had reached her and grabbed her by the shoulders. If he were a different man, she'd have feared a good shaking, but instead, he clutched her against his massive chest. "You're going to drive me to my grave."

"Let's see what is happening in the cellars," Victor muttered. He stepped into the kitchens, was screamed at, and retreated with a torch. They took it outside where Jack called for the constable again.

"Officer Landy? Landy, man! Landy, call out!"

No answer.

"Is he unreliable?"

"Quite the opposite," Jack said. "We should have realized that we were giving the prankster a playing ground when we decided to carry on with the party."

"We're a dim as Denny," Violet muttered as Victor pulled back the cellar doors. The fact they were unlocked was enough for Vi to groan.

Jack led the way down, torch in hand. Victor refused to let Violet go next, but they all relaxed when they heard Beatrice say, "Stop it, you idiot."

Vi gasped and called, "Are you all right, Bea?"

"She's fine. Quite a bump on her head, but she's too hard-headed for a blow to do her much damage," John Smith said, turning up the light on his lantern. "I just found her when I realized that idiot Landy was gone."

"How did you get here?" Vi asked, pushing the rather too attentive John Smith away to free Beatrice.

He handed over his knife and then stepped back when Vi *and* Beatrice shot him a dark look.

"I was stupid," Beatrice admitted. "I saw the letters come in through the slot, and it wasn't time for the mail, so I opened the door and saw a figure running. Who would run but a prankster? I chased her all the way to the museum, to the back gate, and into the cellar where she was, of course, waiting."

"Who is it?" John Smith and Jack asked in unison.

Violet sawed through the last binding.

"I don't know," Beatrice said. "I'd never seen her before."

"Don't worry about it. Victor, help her please. Let's call a doctor."

"I'm fine."

"You need a doctor," John Smith snapped. His pretty angel's face flushed when they all stared at him. "She just doesn't look herself."

"And how would you be knowing how I look?" Beatrice demanded.

"I work for these blokes often enough, don't I?" Smith jerked his thumb towards the others. "I've got eyes. I'm paid to use them. You're pale."

"I'm fine," Beatrice said, as she stood. She lost her balance and Violet grabbed at her, but Smith beat Violet to the rescue. "Just a little off-kilter."

Smith raised a brow at Violet, who shot him a

quelling look before she told Beatrice, "You're seeing a doctor."

"I really am all right," Beatrice replied.

"Then you'll see them for my sake," Violet countered. "It is an order. Remember, I'm your employer *and your friend* and I insist. Let's save the subsequent argument for when you're better since we both know I'll win."

Beatrice didn't look happy, but she nodded begrudgingly.

"Did you see Landy?" Jack asked.

Smith shook his head.

Jack sighed. "Have a look about. Perhaps Beatrice isn't the only one who got hit over the head."

Smith disappeared without answering.

"He's smooth like a snake," Beatrice muttered as Victor lifted her into his arms. Beatrice protested, but Victor ignored her.

"It's our turn to save you," Violet told Beatrice, taking her hand and then turning back to Jack. He'd turned the torch onto the rest of the cellar. Beyond the still-packed crates was a large metal tub. Jack crossed to it and leaned down.

"I believe this is our hundreds of pounds of wine, gin, and bourbon." He gestured to the side and they saw the emptied vinegar, water, and salt.

"The she-devil must have just dumped out some of it and added enough vinegar to ruin what was left."

"I was starting to think it was Danvers," Jack said. "I'm both relieved and baffled. What did you see, Beatrice?"

Jack led the way up the stairs that went inside the house as Beatrice admitted, "Blonde hair, a white face, she got me from behind, sir. It's all blurry in my head."

"Don't worry," Violet told Beatrice. "We'll find her."

"Give her my regards," Beatrice told Violet darkly.

CHAPTER 12

"*B*loody hell, Jack!" Ham said as they appeared in the hall. "Where have you been?"

"The cellars," Jack said as Victor stepped into the hall from the cellar.

"Beatrice!" Ham took in the sight of her as Violet followed, the last to leave the cellars. "Jack. Vi. Damn it!"

"What?"

"Kate, Ginny, Geoffrey, along with Em"—he glanced at Violet, cleared his throat, and amended —"Miss Allen—were too clever for your scavenger hunt. They found your joke, which would have been fabulous if not for the rest."

"And?" Violet asked, knowing that the culmination of the day's events must have come. What would it be? Thousands of beetles? A bag of rats? A room of displays crushed into shards of glass with priceless artifacts destroyed?

"A body."

Violet grabbed Jack's arm before she tumbled back down the cellar stairs and then carefully shut the door behind them.

"A body? A murder? Who?"

Ham paused. "Actually, I don't think it's a murder."

Violet frowned. "Is it a dummy?"

Ham shook his head. "It's quite real. It's just...been..."

"What?" Violet demanded. "Stop softening it for me."

"I think it might be some poor fool who had been donated to a university."

Violet stared, blinking slowly. Then she let go of Jack's arm to shove into the kitchen and take a seat in the corner.

"Don't worry madam," the chef called. "I'll reheat the fish over a cast iron pan. I've made a lemon sauce and vinegar sauce. We'll cut them into bite-sized pieces. It'll be a bit sticky and it won't be stones into gold. Perhaps stones into copper. We'll—"

Vi shook her head. She really might be sick, she thought. Had someone donated their body to a university for students only to end up as the prank of some idiot? She hadn't thought she could get angrier, but she had reached a level of rage where it seemed the blood in her veins boiled. She felt as though she could feel its passage through her temples and at her wrists.

Her heart pounded in her chest in rhythm with the throbbing in her ears.

Jack took her hand, and she glanced at him.

"A body?"

He nodded.

"At my party?"

"Are you all right?" He cupped her cheek and turned her face to his, and then winced at the raw rage in her expression.

"Someone used the remains of a poor soul to *prank* my guests?"

Jack cleared his throat as Violet's nails slowly curled into her palms. Hands fisted, she rose.

"I won't be too slow next time."

"Vi—"

Her gaze narrowed on him. "You should find them first."

"Vi—"

She didn't reply. She strode down the hall towards her friends in the ballroom. If Violet needed someone who would break the law with her, who would set aside all bounds of what might be, then what Violet needed wasn't her beloved Jack *or* her beloved twin. It was Rita and Lila.

VIOLET DID NOT GO HOME that night. She did, however, retrieve her dogs from Victor's house and find her way to Rita's penthouse suite, pausing long enough to ensure that Ginny was all right. Her own private fiend,

Violet thought, when her ward explained that she'd been the one who clued Ham in on the state of the body and the likelihood it came from a school.

Vi pressed a kiss on the girl's head and ordered her to use her powers and intelligence for good before checking the babies before she left.

She arrived at Rita's suite and took one of the four bedrooms for herself and Beatrice. Jack knew where she was and he would find her or not. She wasn't worried so much about that as she was about actually committing murder should she beat Jack and Ham to the prankster.

"I'm surprised Jack didn't appear last night," Rita commented in the morning as she poured herself a cup of tea and watched as Violet started her second cup of Turkish coffee.

"He probably worked all night," Violet admitted. "Especially since he knew I planned to meddle."

"Ham told me to keep my pretty nose out of it or he'd wring my neck," Rita announced as she leaned back to sip her tea.

Violet's head tilted and her gaze narrowed.

"It's like he's daring me," Rita said.

"I've been thinking," Beatrice said carefully. "The ad is still there. The one that seems to have stemmed these pranks. What if we...follow up?"

"How do we even know it is for what's been happening to Vi's house?"

"That snake Smith seems to think it does," Beatrice muttered. "He's not usually wrong."

Violet glanced at Rita, who shrugged.

"I suppose we could find the ad and see if it's something we can answer."

Beatrice grunted, and they both looked at her.

"You can be assured," Beatrice said, "that the snake is doing just such a thing. It would probably be wasted efforts. Forget I suggested it. We might be better served by sticking to our purview."

"Are you saying that we should wait at home wringing our hands?" Rita demanded, aghast.

"No, of course not. Mr. Smith might be smooth in his snakish-ness, but no one can reach the circles you can, Lady Vi. There has to be some rumor of it. Use your connections. Between Mr. Denny, Mr. Algie, the earl, your artist friends, *someone* has to know something."

"She's not wrong," Violet told Rita. "You know," Violet said. "We could get Miss Allen."

"She hates you, Mrs. Vi," Beatrice told Violet flatly.

"But," Violet said slowly, her mouth twisting. "It would sell quite a lot of papers."

Rita looked sharply at Violet, who grinned evilly and rose to make the telephone call.

"You want me to do what now?" Miss Allen asked, glancing between them.

Violet explained for the third time.

"You guarantee there will be prize money?"

Violet bit back the sarcastic remark that of *course* she did, but instead, she just nodded once. Miss Allen looked down at her notes and then again at Violet. "Jack won't like it."

"He'll be fine," Violet said, not liking the light of happiness in Miss Allen's gaze as she said it. Perhaps, Violet thought spitefully, Miss Allen was feeling her years. Violet was, after all, younger than Jack by nearly a decade and Miss Allen was his same age.

Miss Allen's expression did not agree with Violet's assessment, but Vi little cared what Miss Allen thought when it came to Jack. There was a reason, Violet reminded herself, that Jack had ended things with Miss Allen.

Violet spun her wedding ring and waited.

"We're going to have to triple our print run," Miss Allen said. She rose and paused. "I am not your friend."

"Nor am I yours."

"I don't like you."

"Likewise," Violet shot back.

Miss Allen's mouth twisted and then she said, "You did a good thing with Ginny."

Violet's pause was out of sheer shock.

"I met those other girls. Ginny wasn't lying."

Violet adjusted her expression and told herself to think of Miss Allen as she would any other woman. "Yes, I know. Ginny wouldn't lie about that."

Miss Allen's gaze sharpened. "Do you think she would lie at all?"

Violet almost said yes and then thought of her Ginny and shook her head. "Not even about who ate the tarts," Violet said truthfully.

Miss Allen rubbed the back of her neck. "I don't

envy any schoolgirl her life. Not even to have my youth back."

Rita laughed low and Violet glanced her way.

"I was horrible in school," Rita admitted. "It's better to not look back. There's no use in it anyway."

"Agreed," Miss Allen said. She paused once again to add, "Let's not make a habit of this."

"Mrs. Vi," Beatrice said, "I could write letters to your father and Lady Eleanor telling them what happened and asking them to look into things from their end."

"No one else would be better to reach out to the upright elders," Rita told Violet.

"Except, the upright elders would know nothing of this business," Violet answered. "But write them all the same, and make some for Algie and his wife, maybe Jovie and her artist boyfriend? Who else?"

"I know a few adventurous types who might do something like this," Rita said, "though they wouldn't just target you. They might have an idea of who might."

Rita picked up a lap writing desk and left the larger desk to Beatrice. With the scritch-scritch of the pens, Violet thought back to what Miss Allen had said. *Jack won't like it.* After that thought was the memory of Lila. She'd say something to the effect of Denny putting Lila's happiness first and Lila putting Denny's first. Violet was an arrogant wench, she realized as she rose to write a thank you note to Lila, a not-apology note to Denny that repeated he was an idiot, and followed-up with the fact that Violet adored him all the same.

Once she was finished with that, Vi rose and crossed to Rita's closet. They weren't the same size or even close to it, but Violet needed something to wear home that wasn't a costume or a kimono.

Vi dug through Rita's dresses until she found a skirt with a belt, a jumper meant to be loose, and a blouse that was too big but would work under the jumper.

She put her jewelry into one of Rita's handbags and kissed both women on the cheek.

"I'll be back, but I should warn Jack and ensure he has more coffee at the least. I'll bring your clothes, darling Beatrice."

"Are you giving in to the *man*?" Rita teased.

Violet, however, answered seriously. "It's possible that if we want to be happy, we shouldn't worry about the *man* and consider instead about treating the man we love as we would want to be treated."

Rita groaned as Violet blew her a kiss and escaped home.

CHAPTER 13

*O*iolet found Jack at Scotland Yard. She'd switched to a plaid dress, a yellow jumper, and only her wedding ring and one of Aunt Agatha's cross necklaces. With so much consistent hatred, Vi felt as though she needed the memories of Aunt Agatha as a shield along with a dash of faith.

"Vi," Jack said as she walked into Ham's office. "What—"

"What am I doing here? Confessing to my crimes."

Ham cursed and rose to leave the office, and Vi sat down on the edge of Ham's desk to face Jack in the chair opposite.

Violet slipped off her shoes. "Did you sleep?"

"I took Ham home and ended up sleeping on his couch after a long discussion of what was happening."

Violet nodded, unsurprised. "It's hard to sleep without you," Violet confessed. "But I'm here because I put an article into the Piccadilly Press. Em doesn't think you'll like it."

Jack's face had faded to emotionless and even. He could be questioning her about a crime with that face.

"She's probably right," Violet said, propping her elbow on her knees and then her chin on her fist. She liked his face, she thought, even when he was emotionless.

Jack waited quietly, probably intending to use the silence against her, but she had already decided she was going to tell him what she was up to. Silence wasn't necessary. Or perhaps she was guessing on his intent because she felt guilty.

"I thought two could play at the games of hiring random people to work against the other, and I would suspect that I have more money. The article is offering rewards for those who can lead us to anyone who assisted in the pranks or the engineer of this plot."

Jack groaned.

"I asked for information leading to the apprehension of my chronic prankster. They've been directed to the front desk of Hotel Saffron who apparently do whatever Rita wants. Yesterday, she asked them to arrange a hot air balloon for her just to see if they would. We'll be going soon."

Jack closed his eyes and said, "At least you didn't put our address in the paper."

Vi grinned. Then she popped off the desk and straddled his lap. She turned his face to hers like he always did to her and grinned at him. "Do you know I was repentant today?"

"Repentant for your mischief?" Other than general meddling—which she had warned him of—she felt that his statement was out of order and she showed him by pulling his ear. Though it was good to see the glint of laughter back in his eyes. Perhaps he wasn't all that upset over what she'd had done.

Violet watched Jack's eyes crinkle with a smile and she kissed him on his nose. "Lila convicted me in my heart driving me to repentance and confession. Thus my presence here."

Surprise filtered through his grin.

"Do you know what she told me?"

He shook his head, but she could see the interest mixing with the surprise.

"That she and Denny are happy because they put each other's happiness first."

Jack pressed a return kiss on her nose. "I see."

"Are you happy?" she asked him, and he placed his hands on her hips.

"With you?"

"With life," she asked.

"I read your journal. The bit that your prankster intended me to read."

Violet pressed her lips together, realizing what he must have read about and wondered whether he hated what she'd written.

"Do you really want me to stop working for Scotland Yard?"

She considered and then admitted, "I don't know what I want. You being happy is more important to me than anything. Does it make you happy to work for Scotland Yard?"

Rather than answering her, he asked, "Do you like managing your aunt's investments?"

Vi swallowed thickly. She should have known he'd realize her feelings about business meetings and reports. She liked the innovative side of it. Meetings, however, and spoiled entitled rich arrogant men who set aside her thoughts and tried to bully her? It was a waste of time and energy.

"You're training Beatrice for a reason, Vi. You can let yourself step free of the parts you hate."

Vi pressed her lips together, trying for an enigmatic, smooth expression, but she knew she failed.

"Agatha wouldn't want you to be unhappy. You hate those meetings. If the meeting isn't about ridiculous fiction taken far too seriously, it is actual torture to you. Especially without Agatha. It just reminds you of what you've lost."

Vi's mouth twisted and she glanced away.

"Beatrice would be able to tell her family that she was an important businesswoman rather than a secretary. You and I both know she actually likes those meetings."

"She's nicer than me, too," Violet admitted. "I might have scoffed during the last one and then laid my head on the table. Beatrice stepped in and started with, 'What she means is—'"

Jack laughed, but he kept her from looking away when the guilt struck her. Aunt Agatha had trusted Violet with what she'd built.

"This wasn't supposed to be about me," Violet told him. "Are *you* happy?"

"Violet, you make me happy," Jack told her and then answered by kissing her thoroughly until Ham returned.

"This is my office," Ham replied as he came back in. "Go home if you're going to be doing that."

Violet grinned at Ham. "We were just discussing wisdom from Lila and Denny."

Ham snorted. He glanced at them and muttered, "I don't want to hear it. I'm not stopping. I like snorting sarcastically."

Vi grinned evilly. "Rita said the same. Maybe you two really are meant for each other."

"Stay out of it," Ham told Violet flatly. "You're basically a sister to me, Vi, which means I will strangle you almost to death but not quite."

"It's like Rita and I are naughtier together," Violet told him. "Like we've planned something you're going to hate and intend to meddle more."

Vi grinned at him, winked, ruffled Jack's hair just to hear him curse, and left.

She hurried down the hall of Scotland Yard and noticed the streak of desks for the constables who assisted Ham's detectives. There was one fellow who had a bandage about his head.

"Landy?" Violet called.

He turned her way. Violet dodged through the fleet of desks and took a seat nearby Landy. "How are you feeling?"

"Like I got hit on the head with a large branch."

114

"But you lived," Violet told him. "Congratulations. Well done."

He didn't seem amused. She hadn't intended to be condescending, but she thought she might have been all the same.

"Did you see anything?"

"Mrs. Wakefield," Landy told her precisely. "I am not one of your father's servants, and you are not a constable. What I saw and what I know belongs to the Yard."

Violet grinned cheerily at him. She rose, patting his desk. "You've wasted my time, Landy. I won't forget," she teased, winking at him to make him scoff towards her, but she noted the blushing in his ears. Vi really preferred constables who were persuaded by her charms.

She crossed the fleet room and then stood in the doorway and announced, knowing her voice would carry, "One thousand pounds to the constable who discovers who filled Jack's auto with horse feces."

Jack snapped, "Vi!" She heard the laugh in his voice and she grinned over her shoulder at him. "Cheers, darling."

Violet's laugh was drowned out by the clamor of detectives asking Jack if his auto had really been filled with feces. She ran out to the reception desk of Scotland Yard and put both hands on the desk of Officer Kite.

"Hullo," she said merrily to him. She decided to acknowledge the issues that Landy had with her. "I know I'm not a constable, but you are, Officer Kite."

"I am," he said warily.

"What would you say to helping me find the blokes who are harassing Jack Wakefield?"

He grinned at her. "It has nothing to do with them harassing you?"

"Jack's brand new auto was filled with horse feces. Did you know he loves it?"

The constable burst into laughter, winced, and then laughed some more. "I did know." He cleared his throat and attempted a smoothed expression.

"It is funny or it will be when it's all over," Violet told him when he caught her gaze and blushed deeply. "You know what else is funny? Rewards you get for listening to me when Officer Landy refuses to even talk to me." Not quite a bribe, Vi was laying out rewards for anyone who would lead her to the prankster. She wasn't bribing so much as not leaving the constables out. Surely bribing meant trying to get out of a crime you'd committed rather than trying to help find a criminal.

"Landy's a bit of a by-the-book fellow," Officer Kite told Vi. "I'm a little more flexible."

"Especially when there are rewards involved," Vi suggested. He winked and she told him, "I do like you."

"I'll keep an eye out."

"I'd prefer an ear leaned towards the shadier, imaginative fellows who come past your desk. I bet you know more than they realize about them. If any of them help out, they're included in the reward. There's a wide open reward for anyone who can help us track down this person harassing Jack and me and victimizing Jack's poor auto."

He nodded and then leaned forward as he whispered, "How did he take it?"

"Like a man having a tantrum. It was a bit familiar. He may have been imitating me, spoiled woman that I am."

Officer Kite grinned and leaned back with a satisfied expression. "It's nice to know he isn't perfect all the time."

"He isn't perfect all the time," Violet told the constable. She reached out and tapped his desk.

Violet borrowed one of the Scotland Yard's telephones and sent everyone to Kate and Victor's house. She made her way to the house herself, pausing outside of her own home for a few minutes. There was a servant on the front step, standing directly in front of the doors as well as, Vi was sure, another in the back. She had little doubt that her house was as well watched as it could be. Especially with the guard dogs in her garden.

Violet watched long enough for the servant to come down the steps and order the cab to be on its way. When Vi rolled down the window and eyed the man, she didn't recognize him, and he didn't recognize her.

"Out of here, lady. No lurking."

"And if we don't leave?" she challenged.

He shifted his shoulders, which were admittedly quite broad, but he also cracked his knuckles. Vi grinned and told the cabbie. "Two houses down." To the servant running her away from her own house, she said, "Tell Hargreaves to send the chalkboards to Victor's house."

He paused, but the cabbie had already pulled away.

Victor's house also had a servant at the front door. Violet got out of the cab and walked up the steps.

"What do you want?" the servant demanded. He glanced towards her house and then back to her. "I saw you bothering Herbie. You aren't welcome to do the same here."

"I'm Violet Wakefield."

"So?"

Violet snorted and then repeated, "Violet *Carlyle*-Wakefield. This is my brother's house. That house down there is mine. Knock on the door for me."

He moved out of the way and said, "I'm not your servant."

Her head tilted and she told him, "True enough." She reached into her bag, unlocked the front door with her own key, and said, "You're quite rude."

"I was told to be rude."

"I seriously doubt that. Who hired you?"

"John Smith."

Violet grinned as she opened the door for herself. "Smith? Perhaps I was mistaken. Be quite rude."

Violet walked into the great hall as the man bellowed, "Incoming."

Victor's butler came hurrying down the hall as Violet went into the parlor and found that Denny had already gotten the chalkboards into place.

He'd written "suspects" at the top of a board, but Violet shook her head.

"I've clearly infuriated someone. I have some ideas, but let's be thorough. Let's go backwards in time and catalogue all those who I might have tormented."

CHAPTER 14

The chalkboards timeline started with All Hallows and worked backward to finding the snake. Kate was there, along with Victor, Denny, Lila, Rita, Beatrice, Ginny, and John Smith. Vi grinned when she realized that the very fact this particular collection of individuals was meeting to attempt to uncover the prankster had to be mildly irritating to Jack and Ham.

"The most important thing," Violet announced, "is that we figure this out *before* Jack and Ham, given they've abandoned us for Scotland Yard."

"Did you tell them about this little get together?" Lila asked pointedly.

"No," Violet said. "They should know. They're investigators. Also, they didn't tell me about the rude servants at the doors."

"Let's look back," Kate said seriously. "Start from the beginning."

"Obviously," Ginny said, "you had that argument with Mrs. Partridge."

"I've got my eye on Partridge," Smith said. He sniffed as he added, "She's a ripe—" He glanced at Ginny and cut off the curse word. "I've also looked into everyone you mentioned. Your brother could have done it."

"Geoffrey?" Ginny gasped. "He wouldn't."

They all ignored her. "Ginny, of course, but she's obvious. I assume you considered her." Smith added.

Ginny gasped. She glanced frantically at Violet and Victor to check if they agreed.

"Ginny didn't do it," Violet told Smith flatly. "What about Danvers?"

"That man is stark raving mad, Vi," Smith said, and Violet eyed him at the familiarity. "I'm not sure that mice would be his choice."

Beatrice, however, snapped, "That's Mrs. Wakefield to you."

"What are you doing here anyway, Smith?" Rita demanded.

"You're having a meeting about what is happening and I am your best asset."

Violet scoffed. "Go away, Smith."

He rose, eyed Beatrice and ordered her, "Be careful on the stairs."

She narrowed her gaze at him. "Why do you know what the doctor told me?"

"I don't know what you are talking about," Smith

lied and sidled away as though he'd broken into the parlor. Knowing Smith, he might have done just that.

"You should never trust serpents even when you pay them," Beatrice told Violet significantly. "Smith knows entirely too much about the details of our lives."

"Or your life," Denny said. "The man is interested in you."

Beatrice stared at Denny. "Mr. Denny—"

"Let's focus on the problem at hand," Kate suggested like a responsible person. "We've failed on the chalkboards. None of this sheds any light on who might be engineering these pranks except, perhaps, for Mrs. Partridge. Anyone else hates you for a reason you don't know about or they've hated you for so long that they're serving their revenge cold and we won't be able to pin them down without further clues."

Violet groaned. She had come to the same conclusion.

"She's all grown up," Denny said. "This is what's going to happen to Lila, isn't it? She won't enjoy my jokes anymore once we have our perfect tiny devil."

Violet rolled her eyes and then got on with it. "Rita has suggested we follow the advertisement. Everyone we know has their ear to the ground. I think we should take other actions as well. I'm open to suggestions."

"I have another idea," Rita said wickedly. "While you were confessing to Jack, I was not confessing to Ham."

Violet lifted a brow.

Rita lifted a brow in return.

"Stop, we've all given up. All of us. Our idiotic gestures remain. Did you want me to snort sarcastically?"

"Yes," Rita said instantly.

Vi rolled her eyes again. "Tell me what you were doing, please."

"I was checking on where Mrs. Partridge went. Were you aware that Sheila Harris invited her to stay at the Piccadilly Ladies Club after you revoked our invitation?"

"I knew I didn't like her."

"Which means," Rita continued, "that the room she is in is oddly accessible to members of the club."

"Conveniently so," Victor agreed. "It's ridiculous. Let's do this then."

"It's a *ladies* club," Kate told him. "I'll go."

"As the mother of my children," Victor started, "you cannot go. I forbid it."

Beatrice covered her mouth. Violet snorted, and Rita burst into laughter. Lila, however, yawned. Kate crossed her legs, leaned back, and stared at Victor.

"Ah—" Vi's twin said, avoiding everyone's gaze.

"Your voice squeaked," Violet told him.

He gave her a pleading look.

"Probably," Violet suggested, "you're just trying to tell Kate that you love her and you want her to be safe."

"That's true," Victor said desperately. "Also, Ham and Jack will be nicer to Rita and me than a new mother risking herself. Since they don't—"

123

"Want consequences," Rita finished meanly.

"I suppose that's a good point," Kate said carefully, "about—"

"Please don't say consequences." Victor cleared his throat and then rose suddenly. "I'm going to go ask Smith for lock picks."

Violet laughed as her twin left and then told Kate, "You're terrifying to my brother, and I like it." She leaned back as she eyed Rita. "I like how you think. Let's do this."

"We can't until 8:00 p.m. Mrs. Partridge has an appointment with Lady Eleanor Carlyle at that time for a donation."

Violet paused as Rita added, "I might have used your Carlyle stamp to make that appointment, but it is across town, and I suspect she'll wait for a while given the rumors of the Carlyle wealth."

Violet stared at Rita's smirk and then turned to Ginny. "Take note of Auntie Rita and learn from her slyness. Slyness won't lead you astray in life."

"I mean, it could," Kate said carefully, glancing at Violet and then back at Ginny. "Lead with morals and then use slyness as a backup. Err on the side of goodness."

"Lies are a tool," Rita countered. "They are best used with men who prefer purity in their mates."

"Ham won't care that you had previous relations."

"You had sex before marriage?" Ginny asked, eyes wide, expression shocked.

"No," Rita lied. "Of course not. I just want to know if Ham would turn on me."

Ginny glanced between them, looking for lies, and they all put on the same blank expressions. Ginny's gaze narrowed. "I've been wondering. Are cocktails always so bad? I had one at your party, and it made my mouth numb."

"Yes," Kate lied, with a smile. "Of course. We enjoy alcohol for the light-hearted effects, but it does taste bad."

"I thought Victor was supposed to be good at making them," Ginny said, frowning deeply. "Why would he bother?"

"It's a fruitless quest," Violet said. "You can never truly understand a man."

Ginny looked at all of them slowly. "I think you're all lying to me."

"We never would," Violet lied. "Did you want to come with us or go with Geoffrey? I understand that my stepmother is not punishing him in any way for being sent down from school."

"You aren't punishing me," Ginny countered.

"But you aren't a wart like Geoffrey."

"I like him," Ginny replied. "He's my friend."

"Bloody hell," Violet sighed.

"She'll learn," Lila yawned, "or she'll fall in love and put up with his terrible ways like I do with Denny."

Denny gasped. "So mean. You're so mean to me, Lila."

"It keeps you malleable. I don't want to break into Partridge's rooms with them as I'm almost positive Ham doesn't like either of us and Jack is only mildly fond of me. If they wouldn't be kind to Kate, they'd probably jail me."

Violet flopped onto the sofa and propped her feet on Denny. "Move. My feet go there."

"There aren't any other seats," Denny whined.

"This has turned from a family meeting to a ladies meeting. You're supposed to flee with Victor."

Denny shoved Violet's feet off of him and stood with a huff. "You should announce these things. How am I supposed to know?"

Violet put her feet back up on the sofa and told Kate, "You can't come. You're the mother of my babies."

Kate groaned. "You ruin all my fun."

"You did that when you had too much fun and made my babies," Violet told Kate without sympathy. "Lila can't come because she has the other baby inside of her. Victor can't come because he's a man. Ginny can't come because she has to realize that Geoffrey is a wart and not good enough for her."

"*He's* the son of the earl," Ginny snapped.

"It's not that impressive," Violet told Ginny. "You've also met his mother. Those things balance out. Have some pride. Besides, you're a Carlyle now. He's your uncle. You have to call him Uncle Geoffrey to remind yourself that he can never, ever happen."

"He's my *friend*," Ginny snapped.

"No," Violet countered. "Never. Even if he turns fully human instead of one-third human. Go find Victor and have him explain."

Ginny jumped up and stormed out to Lila's low laugh.

"Geoffrey *has* been getting better," Kate tried. There was the sound of an infant crying and Kate cursed and rose, holding both breasts. "I am so tired of them doing that."

Vi and Rita gaped, while Lila asked—horrified, "Is that breastmilk?"

"Yes," Kate groaned. "I'm so tired of ruining my clothes."

"But I love my clothes," Violet said, mouth dropping open. "People should tell you this before you marry. Jack wants children eventually."

"Follow your rhythms closely," Lila advised. "I let Denny distract me and look at me now. Fat."

"At least your ankles aren't swollen," Kate said meanly. "I hate you for your lack of swollen ankles, your lack of vomiting, and your general glow. You make me sick with jealousy."

"I should think you've had enough of that when you were with children." Lila smiled a slow evil Mona Lisa grin and then added, "Overachiever."

Kate gasped and then one of the babies cried again and Kate grasped her chest even more tightly. "It's like I'm a cow." She stormed out.

Rita and Violet watched her leave and then looked at each other in horror.

"It's too late for Lila," Rita said, holding her own chest, "but not for us, Vi."

"It might be too late for me," Violet said, with a frown, hands on her chest. "I *love* my clothes."

127

Lila and Rita gasped. "Really?"

Violet turned and then shook her head. "Not *now*. I'm just saying, Jack really does want children. And Lila told me I have to put his happiness first to have a happy marriage, and I do want to be happy too and maybe that means ruined dresses. I don't know how this works. Why can't they just eat bread and meat when they come out? Somehow Lila has become the expert, and I am confused about the entirety of life now that she's advising me."

"They don't come with teeth," Rita reminded Violet.

"I know," Vi muttered. "I did meet my nieces when they were bloody and slimy. Now that I think back, it was horrible."

"You said it was beautiful," Lila snapped. "You swore it."

"I lied," Violet lied. It *had* been beautiful. Meeting the twins was amazing. Seeing their first breaths, holding them, all of it. It had been haunting Violet, and she was—maybe—ready to have a baby herself. The question was—was Violet going to be pregnant like Lila and glow? Or like Kate and turn into a weeping, crazy, swollen melon?

Lila crossed her fingers over her stomach and crossed her ankles on the table in front of her. "You are lying, Mrs. Wakefield. I know you better than anyone, and that was a lie."

"Except Victor," Rita shot out. "Victor knows Vi better than you as does Jack."

Rita snorted as Violet muttered, "I need a drink.

Did you see what happened to Kate's silk blouse? That was French."

"I did." Rita's expression was mocking Violet.

Vi glared at both Lila and Rita. "We're back to no more lifting of brows, sarcastic snorts, and general scoffing."

Rita rolled her eyes as Lila snorted evilly.

"I hate you all," Violet snapped.

CHAPTER 15

*V*iolet walked up the steps of the Piccadilly Ladies Club the moment they saw Mrs. Partridge leave. The woman at the door opened it so Violet and Rita could walk in without pause. "Mrs. Wakefield. Miss Russell."

"That's Lady Violet to you," Violet snapped. "Where's the management?"

"Not here, my lady," the servant said calmly.

To hide her relief, Vi narrowed her gaze and lifted a brow at the servant.

"I—I'm sorry?"

"You'd better be," Violet said, sweeping in. She crossed to the bar and ordered a cocktail. She sipped it for a few moments, and then made her way up to the rooms, Rita following.

"Did you find out what room it was?" she asked Rita.

"Yes," Rita said. "Are we not sneaking in?"

Violet shook her head. "What are they going to do? Kick us out? We don't really come here anyway. And they aren't going to call Scotland Yard."

"What makes you so sure?"

"Your father's money," Violet shot back. "How are we getting into her room?"

Rita scowled as she held up the key. "Your father is rich too."

"It's all tied up for Gerald," Violet replied offhandedly. "Landy might not be bribed though, so here's hoping we don't get caught and if we do, he isn't the constable on duty."

Rita unlocked the door to Mrs. Partridge's room, and they slipped inside.

"Look for replies to the advertisement lying about. Or items from my house. Or mice."

The room was clean and without personality. The desk itself was clear, but Violet crossed to it to pull open the drawers. She found Partridge's copy of the contract of Ginny's admittance to the school as well as letters from the teachers.

Vi frowned. There was nothing about the pranks. Nothing that led to the Partridge woman being the one who was tormenting Violet and Jack.

She pressed her fingers to her forehead. If it wasn't Partridge, it could be *anyone*. How many times had Violet meddled in someone's life? How many times had she stepped in to help, whether with money or with the determination to find a killer, with no reason to believe that she had any right to tinker in their lives?

"What have I done?" Violet asked. "If it isn't Partridge, then it could be *so many* people. I need it to be Partridge. If it doesn't go back to that one most recent fight, my goodness, Rita. Do you know what I am? What I've done, meddling in other people's lives?"

Rita stared at Violet. "Where is all this coming from? It isn't like you at all."

"I might have gone without sleep when Jack didn't come. I knew he was working, but I couldn't sleep, so I worked on rewriting my book."

"*Why* didn't you just sleep? What is wrong with you?"

"Jack wasn't there," Violet muttered. "I'm dependent on him for sleep now. I'm weak. A delicate damsel who needs rescuing."

Rita scoffed. "This is what comes from no sleep? You're going to be worse than Kate when you finally become pregnant."

Violet jerked at Rita's accusation. "Don't say that. That's a terrible thing to say."

Rita lifted a brow.

Violet groaned. "It's going to be the same with you and Ham."

"I'm not going to lie to you," Rita said, opening the wardrobe and flipping through Partridge's clothes. "You're pathetic exhausted, and just because I apologized on his mirror with used lipstick does not mean I've decided what is right for me."

"You protest too much," Violet told Rita.

"I plan to," Rita said, frowning as she picked through Mrs. Partridge's wardrobe. "There's nothing to see here. Absolutely nothing. It's possible this isn't the person. We did know it was unlikely to think of a schoolmarm putting mice through the slot."

Violet's mouth twisted as she rubbed her temples. "It's possible that I'm a little high strung when exhaustion finally hits me, and I shouldn't have had that drink. This is fruitless."

Violet shoved up from the desk and made her way to the door.

"Let's hire someone to follow her," Rita told her, reaching the door first.

"I thought we already had," Violet said dryly.

Rita shook her head, and then she screamed when she opened the door and found the most masculine, beautiful matron either of them had ever seen.

"Smith!" Rita jerked back. "What are you doing here?"

"I'm here to search the room, obviously. What are you doing here?"

"Same," Violet said. "Are you in love with Beatrice?" she demanded with a hope that the sudden question would trip him into an answer.

Smith was too clever. "I don't believe in love."

Violet's gaze narrowed on him as he pushed into the room and then shut the door. He crossed to the bed and lifted it, looking under the mattress and putting it back perfectly in the same spot.

"Beatrice is too good for you," Violet told him.

"I don't believe in love or relationships. She just

needs to be careful on the stairs. It's a simple precaution."

Violet glared as Smith opened the drawers of Partridge's desk. "I looked there."

"But you aren't me." He slipped his hand into each drawer and felt along the top of the drawer.

"We didn't do that," Rita said. "Feel around on the top of the drawers. We just glanced in."

Smith scoffed, adjusted his wig, and then opened the wardrobe and dug through each pocket, shoe, and hatbox.

Violet glanced at Rita, who bit her lip. "We need to improve our investigative skills."

"You need to stop meddling," Smith told them.

"Yes, we might need to stop meddling," Violet admitted. "It leads to mice in the letterbox and snakes in the library."

Smith glanced back at them. "Or a stabbing in the alley. You're on a quick road to being the next murder victim in Jack's life."

"Mr. Wakefield," Violet snapped. "What else have you learned?"

"Your man-of-business's office was searched. I saw them leaving when I went to search there myself. Too late to follow them, though."

"What?"

"Your man keeps all of his files locked up. Whoever it was didn't get into them."

Violet stared. "Did you?"

"Of course I did."

Violet sighed.

"Your man-of-business is a good man. He doesn't even skim."

Vi glanced at Rita, who said, "Let's just leave. We'll have another cocktail, sleep, and start again tomorrow."

"Do you want to live?" Smith asked.

"What is that supposed to mean? This person isn't violent."

"Tell that to Bea and Landy."

"Bea?"

Smith didn't answer as he ran his hand over the top of the wardrobe and then knelt to check beneath it.

Vi groaned and then called after him, "Stay away from Beatrice."

VIOLET PLAYED with her wedding ring while she tried to decide where Jack would go to sleep. Not Ham's couch again. The hotel or Victor's?

She took a guess and made her way back to her old room and found Jack there.

"I was wondering where you were," he said as she took off her coat and dressed for bed.

After washing her face, Violet drew a deep breath in and then joined Jack on the bed. "I went a little exhaustion-mad today. I'm going need you to breathe deeply, keep your heart beating, and warm my toes."

"I can do that," Jack said, kissing the top of her nose. "What did you find out?"

"Smith is a very attractive, yet still masculine, woman.

135

I was a little jealous of the way his rouge was blended into his natural flush. He is an expert at cosmetics. Far better than I and I've been playing with them for years."

Jack laughed and Violet propped herself up on her elbows. "I don't want you to leave Scotland Yard."

He kissed the top of her head. "I know."

"I just need to try ideas out in my head. I do that in my journal."

"I know that too."

Violet lay her head on Jack's chest and listened to his heartbeat. It was her most comforting lullaby. The thud-thud, thud-thud, thud-thud was music to her ears. She was just so tired and angry. She hadn't been prepared to be so outraged about pranks being played on her. She would have thought that she'd have been able to laugh those things off, but they were so mean.

"How ridiculous is it that I'm mostly bothered by how much this person seems to hate me? Sending out those pieces of my journal to ruin my closest relationships. Destroying Aunt Agatha's china. Burning the newest V.V. Twinnings book. It's so hateful and cruel."

Jack tangled his fingers with hers and lifted them to his mouth to kiss one fingertip after another. "People generally like you. I suppose it must feel odd to have someone dislike you so thoroughly."

"I feel like a whiny little beast that it's affecting me so thoroughly," Violet told him, pushing up on her elbows to look at him. "Broken china and a book that will probably be better when Victor and I write it again. I haven't lost anything that can't truly be replaced." Violet sighed and then asked him, "Who was the body?"

"John Moore. A poor man who couldn't afford a burial and didn't want to burden his wife."

Violet winced. "He knew he was going to die?"

"Of the same thing that seemed to have killed his father. Moore gave his body to science in the hope that his son wouldn't die of the same thing."

"Are they all right?" Violet asked, eyes wide.

"No, they lost their father. But the university doctors who were looking at his body and trying to understand what killed him will be able to carry on their work."

Violet pressed her face into Jack's chest and took in a deep breath.

"How did he end up at our party?"

Jack took in his own deep breath. "A student needed money and saw the prank advertisement."

"What's happening to him?"

"He's been expelled." Jack sighed. "He was bright enough. Just stupid."

Violet pushed up again and met Jack's gaze. "He must have talked to the organizer?"

"He did."

"And?"

"It was a street boy who was paid a dollar for every time he was the go-between."

"And the street boy?" Vi asked, almost painful in her hope that they'd have a clue.

"He's slippery so far, but we'll catch him."

"So it wasn't murder at least," Violet said, relieved. "It's odd that no one has heard anything."

"Yet," Jack said. "Your advertisement goes live tomorrow in the Piccadilly Press. I'm sure that we'll be inundated with useless information and possibly a few gems worth following."

"The Hotel Saffron staff is going to take the information, catalogue it, and we'll bring it to Kate and Victor who are going to use the chalkboards to sort it all. Unless, of course, the party was the culminating event. Then we'll get comfortable again until someone else decides to torture us."

"You are glum," Jack told Violet and rolled her beneath him. "Stop it."

She shook her head, watching his gaze narrow before she reached up and tickled him and saw a shock of surprise on his face. It was all she needed for a full-on attack, which turned out to be all she needed to shake the blues and finally sleep.

CHAPTER 16

*T*he key to shaking the men Jack set to tailing Vi and Rita was stupidly easy. The two women went into a ladies lingerie shop, held up some shocking bits of lace to their chests, and then disappeared into the back of the shop. For a fitting? The men wouldn't know because they couldn't cross the threshold, making disappearing as simple as a handful of pound notes for the shop girl to pretend to bring back more things and a promise to return and spend heavily later.

Really, Violet thought as she eased through the rear door of the shop, you'd think that Jack would have realized they'd shake his blokes. Especially when Jack had included *Landy*. The man deserved the dressing down he was going to get. She sidestepped through the alleyway to the street beyond with Rita at her heels carrying a larger than usual handbag.

"How did you find where to meet the street boy?" Vi asked Rita. "You never said. Did someone answer your ad?"

Rita grinned. "I found the right advertisement and answered it."

Violet jerked with worry. "How were you not recognized?"

"You go to a silent movie show and the person comes and sits behind you. I wore a wig and didn't turn around. I said that I guessed that you were the subject of the torment and that I'd always hated you."

"Did you have anyone with you?" Violet hated that she sounded accusing.

Rita shook her head as they waved down a black cab. "I received a message last night with the showing and the seat number. There wasn't time to get help and make the show."

"You might have called."

"And risked Jack finding out?" Rita gave Violet a smirk and Violet let out a sigh.

Vi slid into the cab next to Rita and they made their way to Hyde Park where the wigged and disguised Rita would meet the street boy. Hopefully, they'd be able to get a glimpse of whoever employed him. A glimpse, Vi hoped, would be all she needed to identify who hated her so much. Wouldn't it? Violet had to *know* the person. Though, as cautious as this prankster had been, it was likely they wouldn't see anyone but the street boy. That might be enough, though, to catch him at least.

They had the black cab stop near the entrance of

the park. Violet got out of the cab and hurried towards the side path that would lead her near where Rita was supposed to finalize plans with the fiend and be paid the first half of the money.

Violet walked from tree to tree. She was wearing a hat low over her head, a plain dress out of character for Vi's usual style, and no jewelry at all. She looked a little like Beatrice and had borrowed her former maid's coat to seal the persona.

Violet stepped behind a tree and peeked out as Rita walked towards the statue where she'd agreed to meet the street boy. No one was there. Violet crossed her fingers and stepped back behind the tree when a hand covered her mouth and she was yanked against a large body.

"I shouldn't be surprised," Jack whispered. "I don't know why I am."

The boy hurried up the path, running with a paper in his hand. He met Rita, threw it at her feet, and disappeared across the garden. Ham appeared on that side and dove at the boy, tackling him while several other men surrounded them.

Jack let go of Violet's mouth. "The men were following your cab," he told her. "You should have gotten separate ones."

Rita leaned down to pick up the note, read it, and crumpled it in her hand.

"How do you know that?" Violet demanded.

Jack scoffed. "You should have realized the moment you shook Landy that it was too easy. We were ready and the cabbie was ours."

Vi groaned and pulled away from Jack, reaching Rita just as Ham did. Vi glanced past Ham for the boy and found the child wriggling and cursing in Landy's grip. Vi's gaze narrowed on him, but Ham was already snatching the note from Rita.

"Nice try?" He cursed nearly as foully as the child, but the boy had a real gift of language. "Damn it! Take the boy back to the Yard, Landy. We'll speak to him there."

To Violet and Rita, he said, "Smith was in the theater. He was able to follow the person who met Rita back to the Hotel Saffron."

Vi gasped. Rita, however, smiled slowly. "The clever beast."

"You both need to stay out of this, Rita. Bloody hell, you're going to get hurt!"

Rita's smile hadn't faded. "Would you care, Ham?"

His curse was the answer Rita wanted as she tucked her arm through Vi's. "I really did like that lacy thing at the lingerie shop. Shall we go back?"

Violet bit down on her bottom lip, unable to call up any kind of amusement. "It's not over."

"No," Jack agreed, his gaze searching hers.

"It's time to set a different kind of trap. We'll need my father."

Jack lifted a brow and glanced beyond Vi to Ham.

"We're doing this," Violet told him flatly. Then another thought struck her. If it were her...Vi turned and ran towards the way the boy had come. She bypassed the obvious paths and saw another form running.

Vi pushed on her speed, but she couldn't catch up. It was like she was chasing a gazelle, and Vi was nothing more than a squirrel. A stabbing pain in her side made Vi stop, but Jack and Smith, in another dress, went rushing past. Their longer legs gave them a better chance, but the form jumped into another black cab, and the driver sped away.

Vi placed her hand on the ache and limped back towards Rita, who lifted a mocking brow. "Don't say a word."

Rita ignored Vi's order. "I thought you were being active daily to help keep your blues away."

"Not as active as that person." Vi dropped onto a bench and looked up at Rita. "Listen—"

"That wasn't Partridge," Rita finished for Vi. "She's way too old and thick to have outraced you like that. Could have been a man."

"She was wearing a skirt."

"So was Smith," Rita shot back.

"Beatrice said it was a 'she' when we found her at the party."

Rita considered this. "Still—"

Ham cursed at both of them when he reached them, but then he said, "I've got to go. Try not to engineer any more trouble."

"We can't help ourselves," Rita told him, patting him lightly on the cheek, and then to his *shock* she kissed him on the cheek.

"Are you feeling all right?" he asked her, stunned.

She grinned. "It's not cat-and-mouse if I don't give you hope sometimes."

He groaned as she kissed him lightly on the lips. "Be safe," she told him.

Rita led the way to the side of the park and then past it to a café. "I need coffee. Did you sleep this time, or are you going to cry again?"

"I slept last night."

"Mmm hmmm." Rita ordered Turkish coffees and scones while Violet stared out the window and watched the Yard men come and go.

"They won't let us play," Violet told Rita. "They know us too well. We need to be entirely unexpected. I have an idea, but you aren't going to like it."

"Why?"

"We're rebellious," Violet said instead of answering. "We're independent women. We do what we want to do and we dress absolutely fabulously while we do it."

"This is true, but what does it have to do with being unexpected?"

"It's time for a garden party."

Rita set her coffee cup down.

Violet nodded. "Precisely. We're going to have to drink tea and wear very large hats with flowers. Parasols. Bow ties. My stepmother the Countess. Her cronies."

"Why?" Rita gasped. Then she paused. "Oh, what a great way to prank you."

"Indeed," Violet sighed. "The worst part is that I'll have to speak to Lady Eleanor and ask a favor."

Rita winced for Violet, who nodded in appreciation and then cut her scone to apply clotted cream and blackberry jam. She took a bite and then told Rita, "I don't want to do it. You ask your father to do it. He'll throw you a big party. He loves you more than my stepmother loves me."

"He does," Rita agreed, "but he's not thrilled that I told him it was his fault that I was targeted by murderous lovers on a ship. He seemed to think it was my fault that Martha told everyone on the ship I was an heiress, and I told him it was his fault he was rich, and then I told him I didn't want to go to Scotland for fishing because I was going to marry a poor police officer who doesn't like bankers."

"Does he care that Ham is poor?"

"Ham's not poor, but no, of course not. My father is somewhat self-made. He started with a rather nice amount from his parents that he turned into buckets of money."

Violet glanced at Rita and then demanded, "Why doesn't he like Ham?"

"He does," Rita said frowning, "and that's the problem. I suspect my father went down to Scotland Yard and introduced himself and fell a little bit in love himself."

"You don't want your father to like Ham?"

"I do. I don't, however, want my father to pressure me about Ham. Because now Father wants *Ham and me* to go fishing with him in Scotland."

CHAPTER 17

"I need a favor," Lady Eleanor said as Violet stepped into her stepmother's parlor. "I'm surprised you came so quickly after I called."

Violet blinked and glanced behind her. She felt as if Lady Eleanor was speaking to someone else. "I also need a favor."

The two of them eyed each other with something akin to resigned distaste. Lady Eleanor had never really liked Violet or Victor. Looking back, Violet could admit that she'd been a terrible stepchild. Violet believed, however, the key description was *child*. Lady Eleanor did not.

"What do you need?"

Violet explained. Lady Eleanor had, of course, heard of Vi's troubles, and Vi didn't miss the smirk that her stepmother had openly cavorting on her face.

"A garden party is absolutely unacceptable."

"It needs to be accessible for someone to slide in who doesn't have the invitation."

Lady Eleanor's head tilted as she looked Violet over. "It is one of *us* doing this to you, Vi."

"Us?" Violet stared at her stepmother. Was she saying that Geoffrey was the prankster? It certainly couldn't be Gerald or the earl. It didn't make sense for it to be any Carlyle but Geoffrey, but Vi wanted to believe her little brother had grown beyond that. Surely he wouldn't have? Not with the body and the horse feces? Surely not.

Still, she had to ask. "Do you mean Geoffrey?"

Lady Eleanor shot Violet a death glare. "Someone connected to *our* world. They knew you'd have your auto brought to the front of your house. They knew you'd have deliveries that would allow them to slide into your house and leave the snake. They knew when the butler would *not* be lingering around the front door for putting mice through the slot."

Violet stared at Lady Eleanor.

"The money to pay for pranks? Only the very rich have that kind of wealth, Violet. Anyone else would throw a drink in your face and spread rumors about you."

Vi rubbed the back of her neck and accepted the cup of Earl Grey tea from her stepmother with the formal politeness required, regardless of their feelings towards one another.

"I thought you were supposed to be clever," Lady Eleanor scoffed. "It's likely enough that your prankster would be invited to whatever party I throw. They may well have been invited to your party, which was *quite* distasteful. Really, Violet. It would be excellent if you would stop making yourself so very notorious. A calm elegance is what is expected from an earl's daughter, even if she had the poor taste to marry a detective."

Violet snapped her mouth shut before she told Lady Eleanor how very much she was despised.

"What do you need from me?" she asked instead.

"Let's save it until after this nonsense is over, shall we? I have no desire to have half your attention when you're so clearly struggling with what should be easy."

Violet set her teacup down with a clink and rose stiffly. "Thank you."

VI TOOK the black cab back to her brother's house and went inside to find the parlor crowded with Kate, Victor, Denny, Lila, and Ginny working their way through the tips gotten though the Piccadilly Press article. Even Vi's little brother Geoffrey was helping. Had anyone thought to mention that he was one of the suspects?

Rita was in the room, but her eyes were closed and her feet propped up. She hummed as she rocked her feet back and forth. On her chest lay baby Vivi and one of the puppies. Kate carried Agatha in one arm while she read through piles of notes from the Hotel Saffron.

"What have we heard?" Vi asked.

"There's nothing useful here," Kate said, shoving a

pile of messages aside. "Silly tips about specific people. There's one for the Duchess of Gloucester. Another for the university librarian. One for a series of school girls. One for that French opera singer. One of the staff of the museum, but they only gave a description of a man who doesn't work for the museum. It's all vague inferences and then questions of when they'll receive their reward. There are also quite a few insults towards you, Vi. People say mean things and we gave them the chance to say them anonymously."

Violet frowned and closed her eyes. "Jack knew, I bet. He knew too well what we'd be receiving."

"Of course he did," Rita agreed. "Ham stopped by, saw the stack of notes, and left laughing."

"This one," Denny announced. "This is the person who did the feces in Jack's auto. Do we follow up?"

"Don't tell Jack," Victor suggested quickly. "That's a job for Ham."

Vi and Victor's gazes met, and they both winced at the memory of Jack kicking his auto's tires.

"Nothing else?" Vi asked, picking up a stack of tips before sitting. She leaned back and flipped through them. Could this be any stupider, she wondered. They were looking for a spoiled rich fiend who had put *mice* through Violet's letter slot and burned her book. "Lady Eleanor says that the prankster is one of us. Because, as she pointed out, *painfully* accurately, only someone as rich and spoiled as we are could afford to do this to us."

"Well, yeah," Denny said, "as the only one in the room who has ever had a job, no one with a regular paying position has the time to spend a whole day dumping out someone else's good alcohol to replace it with vinegar that they would definitely not spend their own money on."

Violet stared at Denny and then glanced at Rita, who nodded. "My father worked as well, and he might have spent money on a prank, but he wouldn't have done it himself. He had to be in the office or building relationships with the crazy rich and well-connected like you people."

"Everyone we know is unemployed," Violet said, considering, "and either heirs of great-aunts or sponging off of those who inherited. Denny does both."

"Have done both," Denny corrected. "I once sponged and then I complimented my great aunt into naming me in her will when my brother was far more deserving. I also sponge off of you all the same since you're still so much wealthier than Lila or I."

Violet rolled her eyes while Ginny bit back a laugh. "Don't think he's amusing, Ginny."

"He *is* funny," Ginny said.

"You like Geoffrey too," Victor said. "He's our main suspect."

"Hey!" Geoffrey complained. "I didn't do it!"

"It's all right," Violet told Geoffrey. "We only think it could have been you because you're clever enough for it."

He stood, offended. "Now I wish it was me. Why would you think I would do that to you?"

"Your mother dislikes me," Violet suggested.

"You're a child. It seems like my own reasoning abilities."

"We also did similar things when we were children," Victor reminded Violet.

"We weren't so mean! I never would have burned her book or broken all of the china she'd inherited from her great aunt."

"You did this to my *mother?*" Geoffrey demanded. "If I'd known, I might have helped. I know my mother is a bit—"

"Mean?" Lila asked.

"Snobbish?" Denny suggested.

"Arrogant?" Victor demanded.

"Opinionated," Geoffrey cut in. "My mother told me that you were inconveniently clever and if you were a man, you'd have been someone to be proud of. She doesn't hate you *that much.*"

Victor choked on a laugh as Violet smacked the back of Geoffrey's head. "What do you mean that you would have helped?"

"I saw the advertisement."

"You know something," Violet said, leaning down to meet his gaze.

He swallowed.

Ginny gasped, and she stood to stare at Geoffrey, gaze narrowed. "He burned Vi's book. It takes her forever to write those."

"He hurt Beatrice," Violet added coldly.

"She," Geoffrey said, clearing his throat. "All I know is that one of the boys from school heard that someone intended to get revenge on you." When

Violet didn't speak, he winced. "The fellow I heard it from is much larger than me."

"On me?" Vi frowned. "Why?"

"It's your fault Ginny went to that school."

Ginny gasped, shooting an apologetic look to Violet. "It's my fault?" Ginny's voice cracked.

"You knew?" Violet shot back at Geoffrey. "You did nothing?"

Geoffrey's mouth twisted. "He's much larger than me and mean. I told you before the fellows at school don't like me."

"You have to quit telling on them," Victor groaned. "I told you that. No one likes the snitch."

"So you tell on the boys at school, but not on those on the train."

"Not Herbie St. Marks. He's huge. He broke Leonard Spry's arm and Leonard only tripped into him. Leonard wasn't even tattling on him or causing trouble or anything. I don't want my arm broken!"

"Herbie St. Marks?" Violet groaned. "Victor!"

"On it," Victor said. "But Herbie really is a beast. Tomas likes everyone, and he doesn't like Herbie."

"Break his arm," Violet told Victor. "Then rub his face into feces."

"I don't think Herbie had anything to do with what happened," Geoffrey said carefully, gaze wide. "I think Herbie *knew* who had threatened you. Father told me not to tattle anymore too, but I told Father what I heard."

"Father knows?" Violet demanded. "What you heard? And he didn't say anything to me?"

"He said he'd look into it."

Vi was surprised by the shock of hurt. She rose and left the parlor before Geoffrey realized how much his statement had wounded her. Violet crossed to Victor's office where his typewriter stood with the new start of their destroyed book. They'd both begun it again, Violet saw, and she smiled sadly at the sight of it.

At least, Violet thought, she'd always had Victor. She heard a creak at the door and realized he'd followed her.

"The dumb boy didn't even realize why you were upset."

"Why would he?" Violet asked, sitting at the typewriter. "He's young. In his head, the world revolves around him."

"He also thinks that the feces in the car, the broken glass, the mice—those are the funniest things he's ever heard. I heard him whispering to Ginny. He doesn't even see how the snake was so dangerous or why you were attached to the china."

Violet sighed and rubbed her brow. "They've both said she. Beatrice and Geoffrey. And I saw her in a skirt when I was chasing her down."

"Yes," Victor said. "Geoffrey pointed that out when you left. Repeated that Herbie only heard someone speaking of it and it was a girl."

Violet glanced at Victor. "Ginny?" But the moment she said it, she knew it wasn't true.

"No," Victor said. "Not Ginny. Someone who hates Ginny."

"From the number of incidents between Ginny and

the other girls, every girl at the school could have been the one."

"Herbie knows which one. I'll put the screws to him." Victor studied her. "Are you all right?"

Violet nodded, but it was a lie. She had been emotional lately, she knew that, but she was so tired of stumbling over dead bodies and seeing the terrible things that people do to each other, usually for some stupid thing like money. She knew she had quite a lot of it and people would think she didn't understand, but Vi *did* understand. She and Victor had barely been scraping by before Aunt Agatha had left her fortune to them.

Before that, Vi had spent her days generally working hard on her books, knowing if she wasn't focused she'd either be eating more eggs and sardines or she'd be forced to marry one of the men that Lady Eleanor threw at her.

Violet frowned and then placed a call to Scotland Yard, leaving a message that they'd found additional information. She stayed in Victor's office while he left to find Herbie St. Marks, their brother-in-law's younger cousin.

CHAPTER 18

"What did you find?" Violet asked the moment Victor arrived home that evening.

"Herbie St. Marks is back to school and has been since before the last incident and so can't be reached quickly. His mother says I'm a horrendous creature and she'll be discussing this with my father. His father says that Herbie doesn't have the wit to have pulled off half the things that happened to you. Mr. St. Marks did, however, laugh until he cried about Jack's auto and the broken lights."

Jack's gaze narrowed on Victor, who flopped onto the sofa and whined, "I need a drink."

Kate rose and made Victor a G&T while Violet sighed. "We knew it wasn't him. We only needed a name. I asked Father over for after-dinner drinks."

"Did he say he'd come?" Victor accepted a lit cigar

from Jack and then crossed his ankles as Jack sat down next to Violet. "St. Marks is a beast. I'd forgotten how much I dislike those of *our class.*"

"Father is coming. He said he *supposed* he knew what this was about."

"You know what occurs to me," Kate started. She rose and left the library where they had gathered for drinks and returned with a few of the tips they'd received. "This tip. The one that said school girls were behind it. Someone had heard a pack of them giggling about mice and pranks and hadn't thought anything of it until the article Miss Allen wrote."

"School girls." Jack huffed his cigar and then repeated. "Spoiled school girls. I suppose I can't beat them, then, even though they deserve it."

"What can we do if it is school girls?" Violet demanded.

No one had an answer.

They had dinner and then waited for the earl to arrive. He came in wearing a fine suit with a cigarette already lit as though he needed it to face them. When he took a seat, he met Vi's gaze. "Now, Vi."

Violet said nothing.

"It's not like you use kid gloves for things like this."

Violet licked her lips and took a sip of the ginger wine that Victor pressed into his hand.

"I don't know which one it is, but I have it narrowed down to two. I've had a word with both of their fathers. It should come to an end and that'll be it."

Violet felt the rush of fury roll up the back of her

neck as she stared at her father. He met her gaze and glanced away. "You have to understand, Vi. These are my cronies."

Vi sipped her wine to keep from lashing out and considered all the different reactions she could have. She could be shocked and horrified. She could simply laugh off the burning betrayal she felt that her father had chosen *cronies* over her and Jack. She could find out which of the she-devils that Ginny went to school with had done it and seek her own retribution.

Violet said nothing.

"Violet?" her father asked. He looked at Jack. "You understand."

"No," Jack replied flatly. "I don't."

The earl turned to Victor, who had the same even expression that Violet had.

"Vi, it's settled," the earl said. "Geoffrey is going to need all the help he can get. These are the folks who could provide it. These are the connections that will get him a position. Your mother is friends with these women, Violet."

"My mother is dead," Violet told him coldly. She rose and left the parlor before she unleashed the full contents of her fury on her father.

He, however, followed. "Don't do anything stupid, Violet. I'm taking care of it."

Violet stopped half-way up the steps and faced him. "I don't trust you to look after my best interests."

The earl stared in utter shock. "Vi—"

"Or even," Violet said flatly, "to give a damn."

"Don't be emotional," he snapped. "You can't expect

people of this caliber to face Yard detectives at their door."

"That snake could have killed Vivi and Agatha."

Her father rolled his eyes as though he didn't think it was a possibility.

"Beatrice and a constable were hit over the back of their heads. A man's remains were moved as a *joke*. A significant and expensive amount of damage has been done to my house and Jack's auto. And things that can't be replaced have been destroyed."

"You can afford it," her father started, and Violet turned from him and rushed up the steps. "Violet!"

She paused without turning. "You should leave."

"Violet!"

Violet didn't stop that time. She hurried into her bedroom, changed into her jiu jitsu clothes and made her way to the ballroom where she practiced the forms she'd learned. She knew she was angry, and she knew she'd been overly emotional since before the pranks had begun. She wasn't sure where the line was between hurt and madness, so she was trying not to think about it at all, throwing herself into her practice with single-minded focus.

Jack was waiting with a glass of wine when Violet finally stopped moving. Her gaze met his, but he was a book she couldn't read. She was just so angry. Practicing jiu jitsu hadn't helped diminish the rage, it had only left her tired.

"Your father loves you, Violet."

She scoffed.

"He's trying."

"If he had said what he knew, you'd already have identified this criminal."

Jack didn't argue.

"And," Violet shot out, "why isn't he bothered? Geoffrey might be too young to realize that someone could have been hurt by that snake, but Father isn't. My goodness, Jack! It was poisonous!"

Jack nodded as Violet paced.

"He has to know that despite being able to afford something we shouldn't *have* to pay to fix our house after some brat destroys things in it! Or your auto! He would be enraged if it was him!"

"I agree," Jack said gently.

"He should care more about you and me than that."

"I agree with that as well."

"I can hear the 'but' in your voice," she accused.

"But," Jack said precisely, "to your father, with his different perspective, he thinks he's protecting you."

Violet scoffed. "I didn't want to sleep in my own house!"

"I know. I don't agree with him. I think it's ill-judged caring."

Violet huffed and then returned to pacing. "He left us wondering!"

"He did," Jack said. "He should have told you that he had a clue and was looking into it. He should have given us the information he had instead of leaving us in the dark. He didn't realize we were staying here. He didn't realize that you couldn't sleep. He didn't know, Vi."

Violet spun on Jack, who held up his hands even

though her rage wasn't directed at him. "He didn't know because he doesn't care."

"You don't believe that, Violet."

"What I know," Violet shot back, "is that Victor and I have always been in last place with my father. I don't expect to be his favorite child. I never have. I'm not even looking for anything other than an acknowledgement that I'm something more to him than his crony's brat-criminal daughter."

"Ham will have a name soon, Violet, but I don't know what we can do with it."

She turned away from him.

"We don't have evidence," he continued patiently, "and no friend of your father's is going to let us question his child into a confession."

"We proceed with the plan," Violet told Jack. "We use Lady Eleanor's party to try to trap the brat who is —obviously—Dorothy Poppington."

"Who?"

"The one who taunted Ginny until she washed Dorothy's mouth out with soap. Her father is Reginald Poppington. Father's long-time poker friend."

Violet took in a slow breath and let it out as she paced. Once they trapped the devil, what was she going to do?

Suddenly, she knew exactly what she was going to do.

Violet patted Jack's cheek as she rushed past him. She hurried out the front door and towards her own house where Beatrice would be working.

The man at her front door stopped her. "You again!"

"This is my house, idiot," Violet told him. Naturally, she hardly looked the part, still dressed in her jiu jitsu uniform as she was.

"Sure it is," he snapped back.

The door opened and Hargreaves started at her appearance. "Mrs. Vi. Get out of the way, Kal. This is the mistress."

"I need Beatrice and coffee in the parlor," Violet said as she entered. "We're looking for a braided school girl with freckles. Look for the sign of the devil on her forehead."

Hargreaves's mouth dropped open, no doubt at the idea the prankster was a school girl. He knew Violet well enough to know the last was an over-exaggeration. Of sorts.

"Are you sure, madam?"

"Unfortunately," Violet said. "If my father or Geoffrey arrives, we're not at home until I tell you otherwise."

Hargreaves's expression had evened out, but his gaze was poleaxed. He simply nodded. "Of course, ma'am."

"Coffee, Hargreaves! I need it desperately. Put something strong in it. Whiskey, bourbon, gin. I really don't care what, but I want it to burn. Oh, and tell that fool at the door to let Rita in."

CHAPTER 19

*T*he day of the party dawned gray and drizzling. The fact that they were having a party at all was utterly ridiculous. The fact that Lady Eleanor had agreed to a tasting party for Mariposa Chocolates sent all of Violet's warning signals flying. Lady Eleanor? Helping Violet with launching something she cared about? The chances of that were very slim. So slim, in fact, that Violet was concerned the favor she promised in exchange was either going to be expensive or illegal. And certainly something Violet would never choose to do on her own.

One of Violet's most recent investments—Mariposa Chocolates—was a business run by a woman to support her family. It was against everything that Lady Eleanor believed in since it meant that a woman could support herself and craft her own life.

The chocolatier was opening a second location in a small boutique in London. Violet had strongly suggested using expensive boxes and gold leaf detailing. They weren't looking to crack into the cheap, chocolate bar market. They wanted to take over a portion of the spoiled artisanal market.

The fact that Lady Eleanor had bypassed her husband's wants to invite Poppington along with the other snobbish, elitist parents of devil daughters from Ginny's school was enough to enrage the earl. Lady Eleanor only patted him on the cheek and reminded him to wear his new fawn suit for the event.

They had caught three pranksters in the process of setting up for the party and Mariposa herself had taken one by the ear—a full-grown hulking man—and walked the bloke to Ham.

Violet had carefully left one chance to prank wide open. It was highly illegal and would require the Poppington brat to act for herself. When the devil child arrived, braids in her hair and wearing a pretty pink dress, Violet put a smile on her face and pressed cheeks with the girl.

"So happy you could come," Violet lied as she shook hands with Mr. Poppington. To Mrs. Poppington she said, "So nice of you to come early and join Ginny and me for our little party. Ginny suggested that you could bring some of the chocolates back to the other girls."

Dorothy's smile went all the way to her eyes and she nodded, blushing lightly. "I'm so happy to,"

Dorothy lied back to Violet with the skill of a profound expert. Her gaze flicked to Ginny, went cold, and then returned to Violet.

"Wonderful. This way, please."

Violet led the way to a large reception room with the most influential guests that Lady Eleanor had been able to persuade to attend. She had a variety of friends who were all quite wealthy, quite well-connected, and quite powerful.

"Are you not coming back to school?" Dorothy asked Ginny. There was a distinct edge of triumph in Dorothy's tone that even her mother noted.

Ginny shrugged and then asked if Dorothy had seen the recent moving picture that Rita had been instructed to attend.

Violet led them into the room, but rather than leaving them, she kept Ginny and Dorothy at her side. "Let me introduce you to my mother, Lady Eleanor. She said she hadn't met you, Dorothy, and I *know* her interest has been piqued."

Dorothy paled and hesitated, but her mother shot her daughter a stern look. No doubt Mrs. Poppington would never allow the chance to pass by for a first-name basis with the hostess of such a well-attended party.

Lady Eleanor had gathered a circle of friends—an actress from America, Rita's elusive but rich widowed father, Algie's bride who made Rita's father look a poor. It was a who's who of influential people.

As they arrived to the group, a waiter approached

and handed each person a small plate of three chocolates with a napkin.

"Oh," Lady Eleanor cooed, "you'll like these.
They're so interesting. Mariposa is a genius."

Violet watched in amusement as Dorothy took her
place among the group and watched the others. The
American actress, a Miss Seymour, popped the chocolate into her mouth and moaned. It was enough for
Dorothy, who imitated the beautiful woman.

The horrific brat met Violet's gaze as Dorothy
raised the chocolate. A smarmy grin crossed her face.

Triumph, Violet thought, as Dorothy popped the
small chocolate in her mouth. It would only take a
moment for the outer coating to melt and the very,
very hot Indian pepper to greet the girl's taste buds.

A quick expression of horror overcame Dorothy.
She choked, and her mother shot her a quelling look
that seemed to declare that if Mrs. Poppington were
embarrassed, Dorothy would pay. Dorothy tried,
Violet had to say. She swallowed the whole chocolate,
tears rolling down her face. Lady Eleanor took slow,
dramatic note, and cut off her ringing comment
midway to lift shocked brows at Dorothy.

Her eyes had developed red circles and the tears
were rolling freely. The girl pressed the napkin they'd
given her to her face and then gasped, yanking it away.
They had, of course, sewed two napkins together, with
chili powder and black pepper in between layers so
when Dorothy pressed the corners of her eyes, they
burned more.

Dorothy gasped into the napkin and got a good whiff of the black pepper and then broke into a row of sneezing that left the horrendous brat breathless and choked. The girl grabbed the glass that was offered to her, pure strong vodka that looked like water, and took a huge swallow, only to choke and spray it across the person opposite.

Lady Eleanor had been told to maintain the position across from the girl, but she hadn't known why.

The scream of fury from the chocolate and vodka shower had every single person in the room turning their direction.

Dorothy's gaze widened, and she gasped through the pain and coughing and spun, fleeing the room.

"Oh, dear," Violet said kindly. "Let me go after her."

In the utter silence, Violet followed the girl from the room and was shadowed by Emily Allen.

Dorothy Poppington had yanked a napkin from a waiter and was wiping her tongue off, crying and snotting in the hallway.

"Oh my," Violet said. "That does look disgusting."

"Your street rat ward did that to me!" Dorothy accused, her voice racked with pain and hatred. "You should throw her back into the streets."

"Oh no," Violet said gently, rubbing the girl's back and waving a servant over with actual water. "That was me, dear."

"You? I'll tell on you!"

"Who would believe you?" Violet circled Dorothy and the girl followed, so they were facing off. Only now Violet was facing the reception room door while the girl's back was to it. "I don't believe your mother or you will be invited back to one of these events. That *is* unfortunate. I understand your mother enjoys lording her position over other people nearly as much as you do."

The girl guzzled the water, used the soiled napkin to wipe her mouth, and then in the habit born of the well-to-do, checked her dress. Her white dress was covered in snot, chocolate drips, and a bit of vodka. She gaped in horror.

"This is called revenge, you horrific brat," Violet said calmly. "Here's a funny thing. You aren't as smart or as clever as you think you are."

The door opened behind Dorothy Poppington and on the other side, Mrs. Poppington, Lady Eleanor, and Hamilton Barnes stood.

"I'm not clever?" Dorothy sneered. "I understand they still haven't gotten the stink of manure out of your husband's car."

"How clever you were in arranging that," Violet agreed. "Your father isn't going to appreciate the bill, I don't think."

"I was clever!" Dorothy agreed. "You don't have proof it was me and you still don't."

Violet shook her head. "It's illegal to do what you did to that man's body. You assaulted a police constable and you kidnapped and bound someone."

"So? No one can prove it was me."

"Proof is much easier to get, Miss Poppington,"

Hamilton said from behind her, "once you know what you're looking for. You were seen by people who aren't loyal to you, miss. They have already made statements."

Dorothy gasped as she whirled around. Her mother stepped forward and slapped Dorothy hard. "You foolish girl!"

Violet had to admit the sound of the slap was almost as good as Jack's heartbeat.

"She deserved it!" Dorothy covered her reddening cheek. "Even you said she shouldn't have sullied my school with that street rat. You—"

"I don't know what you're talking about! Shut your mouth!"

"But!"

"Be quiet!"

Violet nodded at Lady Eleanor and then faced Mrs. Poppington. "You may tell your husband from me and my husband that we will send you the bills associated with your daughter's hijinks. You can count on our discretion assuming they're paid swiftly. Otherwise, you'll be hearing from our solicitor."

Mrs. Poppington grabbed her daughter's arm and yanked her down the hall. Before she got far, Violet called, "If I am the victim of another prank, Mrs. Poppington, all discretion will be lost and you'll discover just what an enemy I can be. Given that I own fifty-four percent of the Justinian Investment Fund, you and your husband should decide what your daughter's crimes are worth to your family's fortunes."

Mrs. Poppington paled and sped ahead. Violet had

prepared for this moment by buying up shares in that fund just so she could have a measure of control. Morals didn't seem to be enough but access to their funds certainly would gather their attention. The barely contained tongue-lashing was nearly as good as the slap, but not quite.

"I would like it noted," Violet told her stepmother and Ham, "that I refrained from wringing her neck."

"Noted," Ham told her. "I'll be sure to put that in my report."

"Is what she did something she'll be arrested over?" Lady Eleanor asked, sounding aghast.

"If she were someone else's daughter, perhaps," Ham said. "I'm sure Mr. Poppington is well-connected enough to hush things up."

Which was why, Violet thought evilly, Miss Allen was standing so quietly nearby. Violet winked at the reporter and stepped back into the room, crossing to Jack and placing her hand on his elbow.

"What was all that?" someone asked.

"It was a thing of beauty," Denny giggled.

THEY WERE USING Victor's auto as Jack's was still being decontaminated and the sight of his old auto made Jack glum. They hadn't gotten rid of it, but going back wasn't what he wanted, and Violet didn't want it for him. Victor's vehicle had been brought around when Violet's father stepped into the hall.

"Was that really necessary? I told you I talked to Poppington."

Violet could have answered so many ways. That Dorothy had tried her same tricks at Lady Eleanor's party. Or that no one had addressed the fact that Violet and Jack were owed an apology and restitution. Vi doubted her father would be quite so lackadaisical about the matter if he realized his household was among the targets.

Or, Violet could have told him that his genuine ineffectiveness in every part of her life left her with a barely functioning trust in regard to herself or her twin.

Or, Violet could tell him that any father worth his salt would have—at the very least—told his child that he had discovered just who was bothering them and would take care of it.

Or, he could have apologized to her for not understanding how much she had been bothered by what had occurred. He could have apologized and told her he loved her.

"Yes," Violet told him simply. "I think so."

The hurt on his face struck her right to her center. The divide between them, the one that had felt like it had been closing, opened wider than ever.

"Goodnight, Father," Violet said and left before she started to cry.

The walk from the house to the auto was tense in the careful silence. Thankfully, however, it was dark so the clever gazes of those closest to her had to judge the riot inside of Violet by the silence alone.

"He's not a very good father most of the time," Victor told Violet, taking her hand, "but he thought he'd done enough. He tried."

Violet didn't really have an answer, but Jack did, taking her other hand in the darkness.

"Vi deserves more than a weak attempt at enough."

"I know," Victor answered as Jack pressed a kiss to the center of her palm, hidden in the darkness.

"You both do," Kate asserted.

"We have it," Violet replied. "Just not from him. Not right now. It's all right, Kate. I can endlessly go back to being grateful that Father essentially gave us to Aunt Agatha, knowing she would do better. He loves us as best as he can."

"And," Victor laughed, "he would have stopped us. He was judging Poppington by what he would do. I suppose expecting from your friend what you would do is reasonable enough."

"He couldn't have known," Violet added, "that Dorothy Poppington was essentially Satan's hand-maiden. I'll send him some of Mariposa's chocolates or something and pretend that everything is all right. We'll be back to normal in no time." She wasn't certain that would happen, but she said it anyway.

Then Vi laughed. "Did you see Dorothy's expression when the hot peppers hit her mouth?"

"It was an act of pure evil genius that you placed Lady Eleanor across from her and gave the girl a flute of vodka." The pride in Victor's voice had Violet snorting and then she lifted a wicked eyebrow despite no one being able to see. Violet relished the freedom of her mocking expression without the gaze of the too-sharp Ginny.

Violet grinned at the memory of Lady Eleanor's expression when she realized what Vi had set up. It had been Vi's own act of revenge for the unnamed favor Lady Eleanor had forced upon her. Vi would keep her bargain, but Lady Eleanor would keep the memory of being sprayed with chocolate, spit, and vodka.

"We're all dressed up," Jack said, knowing exactly what Vi wanted to hear. "Let's go dancing."

GUTTERSNIPE VS. SPOILT BEAST

By E. A. Allen

With the rise of flappers, no one expects anything more than the death of the old-fashioned girl. Sweetness. Modesty. Morals. Relics from the past. Prepare yourself, reader. This is a tale of more than just a girl who drinks and dances until all hours. It's the tale of a child who was rescued from the streets. A child who started with nothing and when given a helping hand, dared to try for something more. Something better. Dared to be hard-working in her new world of spoiled princesses. One would hope that this would be the start of Cinderella's rising, but no. It's a dichotomous tale of the girl from the streets and the girl with the silver spoon. Read on and see for yourself. Judge for yourself—

VIOLET CLOSED the paper and handed it to Ginny. "Jack and Victor are driving you to that school, my sweet criminal. Jack isn't going to miss anything that seems awry. And Victor is going to trap you in promises of hard work and examine all the ways you could slip out of classes."

"You would have slipped out of classes," Ginny said carefully. Her gaze widened on the article in the Piccadilly Press. Her mouth dropped open as she realized that once again, she was in the papers and this time Dorothy Poppington hadn't been referred to in vague asides.

Violet placed a gentle hand on the paper and leaned in. "*I* didn't want to be a doctor. You've crafted bigger dreams than I."

Ginny understood and she nodded.

"If you're going to rise up," Violet told her, "you rise up every day. It isn't a choice we make one time."

"I will," Ginny said. "You can trust me."

"I know," Violet agreed, standing to put a kiss on the girl's head.

"I'll be better than you would have been," Ginny said with a mocking laugh as Violet went to leave the breakfast room

"Easily done," Violet said with a laugh of her own. "Victor and I set something of a low bar. Try to rise a little higher than we did."

Ginny lifted a daring brow and winked. With a merry grin, she returned to the paper and missed seeing Violet's wince. Really, Violet thought, they'd set so many low bars.

The End

HULLO FRIENDS! Once again, it's my chance to tell you how much I appreciate you reading my books and giving me a chance. If you wouldn't mind, I would be so grateful for a review.

THE SEQUEL to this book is available now.

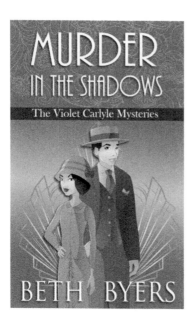

November 1925

Violet and Jack are called to London by the most unexpected of people--Lady Eleanor. She's in trouble and when the chips are down, she turns for the help to the stepdaughter she'd alienated and the son-in-law that she's despised.

Will they find it within themselves to help her? And if so, what will they do with what they find?

Order your copy here.

The newest Poison Ink Mystery is also available now.

September 1937

Georgette Dorothy Aaron is expecting a bundle of joy, focusing on updating her house, writing books, and enjoying her family. What she's not doing is meddling. She's not sticking her nose in other people's business. She's not writing books about her neighbors. She's determined to turn over a new leaf and slide right back into the safety of being a wallflower.

Georgette, however, gets stuck on her book, sick of the smell of drying paint, and decides to take a ramble. When she stops to check herself in the mirror, she doesn't expect to see someone *else* in the reflection. Nor does she expect what happens next.

Order your copy here.

A new paranormal 1920s series is now available.

April 1922

When the Klu Klux Klan appears at the door of the
Wode sisters, they decide it's time to visit the ancestral
home in England.

With squabbling between the sisters, it takes them too
long to realize that their new friend is being haunted.
Now they'll have to set aside their fight, discover just
why their friend is being haunted, and what they're
going to do about it. Will they rid their friend of the
ghost and out themselves as witches? Or will they look
away?

Join the Wode as they rise up and embrace just who

and what they are in this newest historical mystery adventure.

Order your copy here.

There is also a new 1920s series about two best friends, written by one of my best friends and I. If you'd like to check it out, keep on flipping for the first chapter.

July 1922

If there's one thing to draw you together, it's shared misery.

Hettie and Ro married manipulative, lying, money-grubbing pigs. Therefore, they were instant friends.

When those philandering dirtbags died, they found themselves the subjects of a murder investigation. Did they kill their husbands? No. Did they joke about it? Maybe. Do they need to find the killer before the crime is pinned on them? They do!

Join Hettie and Ro and their growing friendship as they delve into their own lives to find a killer, a best friend, and perhaps a brighter new outlook.

Order your copy here.

ALSO BY BETH BYERS

THE VIOLET CARLYLE COZY HISTORICAL
MYSTERIES

Murder & the Heir

Murder at Kennington House

Murder at the Folly

A Merry Little Murder

New Year's Madness: A Short Story Anthology

Valentine's Madness: A Short Story Anthology

Murder Among the Roses

Murder in the Shallows

Gin & Murder

Obsidian Murder

Murder at the Ladies Club

Weddings Vows & Murder

A Jazzy Little Murder

Murder by Chocolate

Candlelit Madness: A Short Story Anthology

A Friendly Little Murder

Murder by the Sea

Murder On All Hallows

Murder in the Shadows

A Jolly Little Murder

Christmas Madness: A Short Story Anthology

Hijinks & Murder

Love & Murder

A Zestful Little Murder (coming soon)

A Murder Most Odd (coming soon)

Nearly A Murder (coming soon)

THE HETTIE AND RO ADVENTURES

co-written with Bettie Jane

(This series is complete.)

Candlelit Madness (prequel short story)

Philanderers Gone

Adventurer Gone

Holiday Gone

Aeronaut Gone

THE POISON INK MYSTERIES

Death by the Book

Death Witnessed

Death by Blackmail

Death Misconstrued

Deathly Ever After

Death in the Mirror

A Merry Little Death

THE 2ND CHANCE DINER MYSTERIES

(This series is complete.)

Spaghetti, Meatballs, & Murder

Cookies & Catastrophe

Poison & Pie

Double Mocha Murder

Cinnamon Rolls & Cyanide

Tea & Temptation

Donuts & Danger

Scones & Scandal

Lemonade & Loathing

Wedding Cake & Woe

Honeymoons & Honeydew

The Pumpkin Problem

PREVIEW OF PHILANDERER GONE

CHAPTER ONE

*T*he house was one of those ancient stone artisan-crafted monstrosities that silently, if garishly, announced out and out *buckets* of bullion, ready money, the green, call it what you would, these folks were simply rolling in the good life. The windows were stained glass with roses and stars. The floor was wide-planked dark wood that was probably some Egyptian wood carried by camel and horse through deserts to the house.

Hettie hid a smirk when a very tall, beautiful, uniformed man slid through the crowd and leaned down, holding a tray of champagne and cocktails in front of her with a lascivious gaze. She wasn't quite sure if he appreciated the irony of his status as human art for the party, or if he embraced it and the opportunity it gave him to romance bored wives.

She was, very much, a bored wife. Or, maybe disillusioned was the better word. She took yet another flute of champagne and curled into the chair, pulling up her legs, leaving her shoes behind.

The sight of her husband laughing uproariously with a drink in each hand made her want to skip over to him and toss her champagne into his face. He had been drinking and partying so heavily, he'd become yellowed. The dark circles under his eyes emphasized his utter depravity. Or, then again, perhaps that was the disillusionment once again. Which came first? The depravity or the dark circles?

"Fiendish brute," Hettie muttered, lifting her glass to her own, personal animal. Her husband, Harvey, wrapped his arm around another bloke, laughing into his face so raucously the poor man must have felt as though he'd stepped into a summer rainstorm.

"Indeed," a woman said and Hettie flinched, biting back a gasp to twist in the chair and see who had overheard her.

What a shocker! If Hettie had realized that anyone was around instead of a part of that drunken sea of flesh, she'd have insulted him non-verbally. It was quite satisfying to speak her feelings out loud. Heaven knew he deserved every ounce of criticism. She had nothing against dancing, jazz, cocktails, or adventure. She did, however, have quite a lot against Harvey.

He had discovered her in Quebec City. Or rather he'd discovered she was an heiress and then pretended to *discover* her. He'd written her love letters and poems, praising her green eyes, her red hair, and her pale skin as though being nearly dead-girl white were something to be envied. He'd made her feel beautiful even though she tended towards the plump, and he'd seemed oblivious to the spots she'd been dealing with on her chin and jawline through all of those months.

A fraud in more ways than Hettie could count, he'd spent the subsequent months prostrating himself at her feet, romancing her, wearing down her defenses until she'd strapped on the old white dress and discovered she'd gotten a drunken, spoiled, rude, lying ball and chain.

"Do you hate him too?" Hettie asked, wondering if she were commiserating with one of her husband's lovers. She would hardly be surprised.

"Oh so much so," the woman said. Her gaze met Hettie's and then she snorted. "Such a wart. Makes everything a misery. It's a wonder that no one has clocked him over the back of the head yet."

Hettie shocked herself with a laugh, totally unprepared to instantly adore one of her husband's mistresses, but they seemed to share more than one thing in common. "If only!"

She lifted her glass in toast to the woman, who grinned and lifted her own back. "Cheers, darling."

"So, are you one of his lovers?" the woman asked after they had drunk.

"Wife," Hettie said and the woman's gaze widened.

"Wife? I hardly think so."

"Believe me," Hettie replied. "I wish it wasn't so."

"As his wife," the woman said with a frown, "I fear I must dispute your claim."

Hettie's gaze narrowed and she glanced back at Harvey. His blonde hair had been pomaded back, but some hijinks had caused the seal on the pomade to shift and it was flopping about in greasy lanks. He had a drink in front of him and the man he'd been molesting earlier had one as well. The two clanked their glasses together and guzzled the cocktails. Harvey leaned into the man and they both laughed raucously.

"Idiot," the woman said. "Look at him gulping down a drink that anyone with taste would have sipped. The blonde one, he must be yours?"

Hettie nodded with disgust and grimaced. "Unfortunately, yes, the blond wart with the pomade gone wrong is my unfortunate ball and chain. So the other fool is yours?"

The woman laughed. "I suppose I sounded almost jealous. I wasn't, you know. I'd have been happy if Leonard was yours."

"Alas, my fate has been saddled with yon blonde horse, Harvey."

They grinned at each other and then the other woman held out her hand. "Ro Lavender, so pleased to meet someone with my same ill-fate. Makes me feel less alone."

Hettie looked at that fiend of hers, then held out her own hand. "Hettie Hughes. I thought Leonard's last name was Ripley."

"Oh, it is," Ro said. "I try not to tie myself to his wagon unless it benefits me. At the bank, for instance."

Ro was a breath of fresh air. Hettie decided nothing else would do except to keep her close. "Shall we be bosom friends?" Hettie asked.

"I just read that book," Ro said. "Do you love it as well?"

"I'm Canadian," Hettie replied, standing to twine her arm through Ro's. "Of course I've read it. Anne, Green Gables, Diana, Gilbert, Marilla, and Prince Edward Island were fed to me with milk as a babe. Only those of us with a fiendish brute for a husband can truly understand the agony of another. How did you get caught?"

"Family pressure. We were raised together. Quite close friends over the holidays, but I never knew the real him until after."

Hettie winced. "Love letters for me," she said disgustedly. "You'd think modern women such as ourselves wouldn't have been quite so…"

"Stupid," Ro replied, tucking her bobbed hair behind her ear.

The laughter from the crowd around the table became too much to hear anything and Hettie raised her voice to ask, "Why are we here? Shall we escape into the nighttime?"

"Let's go to Prince Edward Island," Ro joked. "Is it magical there? I've always wanted to go."

"I've never been," Hettie admitted, "but I have a sudden desperate need. Let's flee. You know they won't miss us until their fathers insist they arrive with their respectable wives on their arms."

"Or," Ro joked, "I could murder yours and you could murder mine, and we could create our freedom. If our families want respectable, I would definitely respect a woman that could rid herself of these monsters."

"That sounds lovely. Until we can plan our permanent freedom, I suppose our best option is simply to disappear into the night."

Ro lifted her glass in salute and sipped.

Hettie set aside her champagne flute, slipped on her shoes, and then turned to face her husband, who had pulled Mrs. Stone, the obvious trollop, into his lap and was kissing her extravagantly. Hettie scrunched up her nose and gagged a little. Mrs. Stone had been in Nathan Brighton's lap last week.

"She slept with Leonard too," Ro informed Hettie with an even tone.

Hettie reveled in the camaraderie she found in Ro's resigned tone. "Have you met Mr. Stone?"

Ro nodded. "He doesn't realize. He's not the type of man to be cuckolded like this. So...overtly. Have you heard of the marriage act they've proposed?"

Hettie nodded with little doubt that her eyes had brightened like that of a child at Christmas. "I will be there on the very first day. If Harvey had any idea, any at all, he'd be rolling over in his future grave. The money's mine, you know? My aunt never liked Harvey and she tied up my money tightly. He gets what he wants because it's easier to give it to him than listen to him whine, but he won't get a half-penny from me the day I can file divorce papers. They say it's going to go through."

"I couldn't care less about the money," Ro replied. "Though my money is coming from a still-living aunt. Leonard has enough, I suppose, but his eye is definitely on Aunt Bette's fortune."

"So," Hettie joked, "he needs to go before she does."

Ro choked on a laugh and cough-laughed so hard she was wiping away tears.

"Darling!" Harvey hollered across the room. "We're going down to Leonard's yacht. You can get yourself home, can't you?"

Hettie closed her eyes for a moment before answering. "Of course I can. Don't fall in." She crossed her fingers so only Ro could see. Ro's laugh made Hettie grin at Harvey. He gave her a bit of a confused look. Certainly he had shouted his exit with the hope she wouldn't scold him. Foolish man! She'd welcome him moving into Mrs. Stone's bed permanently and leaving his wife behind.

The handsome servant from earlier picked up Hettie's abandoned glass and shot her a telling, not quite disapproving look.

"Oh ho," Hettie said, making sure the man heard her. "We've been overheard."

"We've been eavesdropped," Ro agreed. Then with a lifted brow to the human art serving champagne, she said, "Boy, our husbands are aware of our lack of love. There's no chance for blackmail here."

"Does your aunt feel the same?" he asked insinu-atingly.

Hettie stiffened, but Ro simply laughed. "Do you think she hasn't heard the tale of that lush Leonard? She's written me stiff upper lip letters. Watch your step and your mouth or you'll lose your position despite your pretty face. It doesn't matter how you feel, only how you look. No one is paying you to think."

The servant flushed and bowed deeply, shooting them both a furious expression before backing away silently.

"Cheeky lad," Hettie muttered. "You scolded him furiously. Are you sure you weren't letting out your rage on the poor fellow?"

"Cheeky yes," Ro agreed. She placed a finger on her lip as she considered Hettie's question and then agreed. "Too harsh as well. I suppose I would need to apologize if he didn't threaten to blackmail me."

"But pretty," they said nearly in unison, then laughed as the servant overhead them and gave them a combined sultry glance.

"No, no, boyo," Ro told him. "Toddle off now, darling. We've had quite our fill of philandering, reck-less men. You've missed your window." Ro's head cocked as she glanced Hettie over. "Shall we?"

"Shall we what, love?"

Ro grinned wickedly. "Shall we be bosom friends then? Soul sisters after one shared breath?"

"Let's," Hettie nodded. "As the man I thought was

my soulmate was an utter disaster, I'll take a soul sister as a replacement."

They sent a servant to summon Hettie's driver. "I was thinking of going to a bottle party later. At a bath house? That might distract us."

Hettie cocked her head as she considered. "Harvey *does* expect me to go home."

Ro lifted her brows and waited.

"So we must, of course, disillusion him as perfectly as he has me."

"There we go! It's only fair," Ro cheered, shaking her hands over her head. "I have been considering a trip to the Paris fashion salons."

"Yes," Hettie immediately agreed, knowing it would enrage Harvey, who preferred her tucked away in case he wanted her. "We should linger in Paris or swing over to Spain."

"Oooh, Spain!"

"Italy," Hettie suggested, just to see if Ro would agree.

"Yes!"

"Russia?"

Ro paused. "Perhaps Cote d'Azur? Egypt? Somewhere warmer. I always think of snow when I think of Russia, and I only like it with cocoa and sleigh rides. Perhaps only one or two days a year."

"Agreed—" Hettie trailed off, eyes wide, as she saw Mrs. Stone enthusiastically kiss the cheeky servant from earlier and then adjust her coat. She winked at Hettie on the way out, caring little that both of them knew Mrs. Stone would be climbing into Harvey's bed later. Or, perhaps it was Harvey who would be climbing into *Mr.* Stone's bed. "Is her husband really blind to it?"

"Oh yes," Ro laughed. "He's quite a bit older you know, and even more old-fashioned than my grandfather. He's Victorian through and through. He probably has a codicil in the will about her remarrying. The type of things that cuts her off if she doesn't remain true to him. Especially since he's in his seventies, and she's thirty? Perhaps?"

Hettie shook her head. "They have a rather outstanding blackberry wine here," she said, putting Mrs. Stone out of her mind. "Shall we—ah—borrow a bottle or two?"

Ro nodded and walked across to the bar. She dug through the bottles and pulled out a full bottle of blackberry wine, another of gin, and a third of a citrus liqueur. "Hopefully someone will think to bring good mixers." She handed one of the bottles to Hettie before tucking one under each arm.

The butler eyed them askance as they asked for their coats.

"Don't worry, luv," Ro told the butler. "Your master doesn't mind."

None of them believed that whopper of a lie, but Ro's cheerful proclamation made it seem acceptable.

"Thief," Hettie hissed innocently as her driver, Peterson, opened the door for them and they dove inside. She struggled with the cork and then asked, "Are we going nude or shall we grab bathing costumes?"

"My brother-in-law lives with us," Ro said, looking disgusted, "I'll be going nude before I go back and face that one. Look—" Her head cocked as the black cab sped up. "I think that's him! We can rush back to collect my bathing costume before he returns to the house."

"I'm a bit too round to want to go full starkers."

"The men love the curves," Ro told her. "If you wanted to step out on your Harvey, you'd need to up the attitude and cast a come hither gaze."

"Like this?" Hettie asked, attempting one but feeling as though she must look like she had something in her eye.

"Like this," Ro countered, glancing at Hettie out of the corner of her eye. "I'm thinking of a really nice plate of biscuits."

Hettie tried it and Ro bit back a laugh. "Are you angry with the biscuits?"

"Let me try imagining cakes. I do prefer a lemon cake." Hettie glanced at Ro out of the corner of her eye, imagining a heavily iced lemon cake, and then smiled just a little.

"No, no," Ro said, showing Hettie again what to do.

"Oh! I know." Hettie imagined the divorce act that Parliament was considering.

"Yes! Now you've got it! Was it a box of chocolates?"

Hettie confessed, sending Ro into a bout of laughter and tears that saw them all the way to Hettie's hotel room. From her hotel room to Ro's house, there were random bursts of giggles and stray tears. Once they reached to bath house, Ro said, "I'll be drinking to that divorce act tonight. Possibly for the rest of my life."

"If it frees me," Hettie told Ro dryly, "I'd paper my house with a copy of it to celebrate those who saved us from a fate I should have known better than to fall into."

ORDER YOUR COPY HERE.

Printed in Great Britain
by Amazon

17886894R00120